PEN PALS:
BOOK SIXTEEN

BOY CRAZY

by Sharon Dennis Wyeth

A YEARLING BOOK

Published by
Dell Publishing
a division of
Bantam Doubleday Dell Publishing Group, Inc.
666 Fifth Avenue
New York, New York 10103

The trademark Yearling ® is registered in the U.S. Patent and Trademark Office.
The trademark Dell® is registered in the U.S. Patent and Trademark Office.
ISBN: 0-440-40426-6

Published by arrangement with Parachute Press, Inc.
Printed in the United States of America
March 1991
10 9 8 7 6 5 4 3 2 1
OPM

For Marc Dennis

CHAPTER ONE

"Thirty-two, thirty-three, thirty-four . . ." Palmer Durand sat cross-legged on the floor of the sitting room of Suite 3-D, counting the collection of brightly colored envelopes that surrounded her. Her golden hair gleamed in the afternoon sunlight. All of the envelopes were addressed to Palmer. "Thirty-five . . ." she continued, looking up as her suitemate Shanon Davis said something unintelligible. "What did you say?" Palmer asked.

Shanon brushed a strand of sandy brown hair out of her eyes. " *'O tempora! O mores!'* " she replied.

Palmer gave a dramatic sigh. "I was afraid it was something like that."

"Hmm-nh," Shanon murmured without lifting her eyes from her Latin book. She was curled up on the pink loveseat, her open book balanced on one knee, a half-eaten pear on the other.

"Well?" Palmer said, a little impatiently. She hated to be ignored. "What does it mean anyway?"

" 'O the times, O the morals,' " Shanon translated. "It's Cicero."

"Well, Cicero just made me lose count," Palmer said crossly.

"Sorry."

Palmer frowned at her suitemate. All of the fourth-formers at the Alma Stephens School for Girls, a private boarding school in New Hampshire, had to take Latin, but Shanon was the only person she knew who actually *liked* it. Then again, Shanon always got A's in Latin, while Palmer was barely making a D. "I thought you already finished this week's assignment," she said.

"I did."

"Then what are you doing?"

"Next week's assignment."

"Tell me you're putting me on," Palmer begged. "Please tell me my own suitemate isn't working *ahead* in Latin."

"I like it," Shanon said simply.

"You're not supposed to like Latin," Palmer explained. "No one is supposed to like Latin. It's a sin punishable by death."

The door to the suite opened and Palmer's roommate, Amy Ho, swept in, a red baseball cap perched on her jet-black hair.

Shanon looked up and grinned. "How's the softball team?"

Amy gave her a thumbs-up sign. "Two and 0 and heading for a sweep. Coach says we're the best team Alma's ever had." She pulled off her black leather jacket. Underneath it she wore black nylon cycling shorts, a black cutoff T-shirt, and black high tops with red laces and red socks. "I know we've only played two games, but so far it's pretty amazing. Sometimes we're all so keyed into each other, it's like ESP or something."

2

Palmer rolled her eyes. She was on Alma's tennis team, which just might be the worst team in the history of the school. Make that the history of the world. The last thing she wanted to do was listen to Amy boast about how hot the softball team was. "Doesn't anybody want to know what I'm doing?" she said, determined to change the subject.

Amy looked at her coldly and turned away.

And Palmer knew why. Not long ago, Amy, who dreamed of being a rock singer, had tried to join a local band run by an older boy named Emmett. Palmer had known from the start that Emmett was bad news. Amy hadn't wanted to listen, so Palmer had . . . well . . . taken the matter into her own hands for Amy's own good. Now Amy wasn't in Emmett's band and she blamed Palmer. "Look," Palmer said patiently. "You've got to get over Emmett. I mean, he is a total creep. He stole one of your songs. You ought to be glad I helped you get him out of your life."

Totally exasperated, Amy turned toward Shanon. "Will you please tell Palmer that I don't appreciate anyone—especially my roommate—trying to run my life?"

"I heard you, I heard you," Palmer moaned. She couldn't understand why Amy was holding such a grudge.

Shanon closed her Latin book. "Let's pretend I didn't hear any of that," she said in a deliberately cheerful tone. Of the four suitemates, Shanon was the one who always tried to make peace. She refused to take sides in the cold war between Palmer and Amy. She glanced curiously at Palmer's pile of envelopes. "What are you doing?"

"Counting all the letters from my pen pals," Palmer replied with satisfaction. "I'm already up to thirty-five, and

3

I haven't even counted the ones from Sam." She pointed to a thick pile of off-white envelopes labeled *O'Leary* in big, bold script. Sam O'Leary was Palmer's main pen pal, and she was crazy about him. He was the drummer and lead singer for his band, Sam and The Fantasy. Plus he was exceptionally cute and wrote great letters.

"Why are you counting them?" Shanon asked.

"Well, I took them out to show Germaine and Reid," Palmer explained. "I'm trying to convince them to get pen pals, too. I think I'm going to place an ad in the Ardsley *Lion* for them."

"Germaine and Reid?" Shanon echoed in disbelief.

"Why would you want to do anything for those two snobs?" Amy asked.

"I happen to like Germaine and Reid," Palmer said defensively. "You two are the snobs. You just won't give them a chance."

Shanon looked as if she was going to say something and then changed her mind. "Are you sure you're not advertising for more pen pals for yourself?" she asked.

At the beginning of their first year at Alma, the girls had advertised for pen pals at Ardsley, the nearby boys' school. They placed their ad in the Ardsley *Lion* under the name "Foxes of the Third Dimension," and now they were Foxes forever.

Palmer smiled smugly. "I've got all the pen pals I can handle right now. Besides, things are going great with Sam. He's going to take me to the B-52's concert. I wrote him a letter last week and asked him to. You're going, aren't you?"

"Are you kidding?" Shanon replied. "Those tickets sell for thirty dollars apiece."

4

"So?" Palmer said. "Tell Mars to take you."

Shanon stared at her suitemate in amazement. Her family lived in town and couldn't afford to send her to Alma. She'd been lucky to win a scholarship. No matter how long she knew Palmer, she couldn't get used to the way her suitemate took money for granted. "Even if Mars's family has money," she explained, "I can't ask him to lay out sixty dollars."

"Of course you can," Palmer said cheerfully. "Really, Shanon, you have a lot to learn about boys."

"I would learn it from someone else if I were you, Shanon," Amy observed.

"That does it," Palmer said, standing up. "I have been as nice and polite as I can be, Amy Ho. You have no right to be so rude to me!"

Amy lifted one eyebrow skeptically, and began to make her way through the maze of letters toward the room she shared with Palmer "Good grief," she muttered, "this room is getting smaller and smaller."

"I think it's okay," Shanon replied weakly. "It's the same size it always was."

"But there's definitely a lot more stuff in it," Palmer added, not willing to let the argument drop. "Everywhere I look, I see junk." She eyed Amy's guitar case and catcher's mitt in the corner. "Whose stuff is that?" she asked in mock innocence.

Amy scowled at her but didn't respond. Picking up her mitt and guitar case, Amy spoke to Shanon again. "Please tell Palmer that if she's bothered by my stuff, all she has to do is ask me to move it."

"Did you hear that?" Shanon asked wearily.

"Yes, I heard it," Palmer responded with a huff. "And

5

you can tell Amy for me that if she thinks my letters and other belongings are junk, she can say it to my face. Of course," she added, "I can understand how seeing all the letters from my pen pals might upset her, since her own pen pal, John Adams, dumped her!"

"Tell Palmer he did *not* dump me!" Amy stated in icy tones.

"That's the way it seemed to me," Palmer said sweetly. "And all because you were so wired to play rock and roll with that loser, Emmett. By the way," she added, "are you still writing to him?"

Amy turned to Shanon once again. "Will you tell Miss Busybody Durand that it's none of her business?"

Exasperated, Shanon threw up her hands, sending her pear flying. "Stop it, both of you!" She stomped across the room to retrieve the pear. "It's too nice a day to be arguing. Why don't we all go out for sodas and cool off?"

Both Palmer and Amy glared at her. "It won't work," Amy said finally. "I can't have a normal conversation with that girl."

"I agree completely," Palmer said. "Now if you don't mind, I have something important to do." She went back to counting her letters.

"So do I," Amy said, stalking into their room and slamming the door.

"This is awful," Shanon said in despair.

"I wonder how I should phrase the ad," Palmer mused. " 'Wanted: Boy Correspondents' or 'Girls desire to make acquaintances of boys through letters' or 'Boys Wanted!' . . . I think 'Boys Wanted!' is best, don't you?"

"It's okay, I guess," said Shanon, still upset.

"Did I show you these?" Palmer held up two letters

written on graph paper and pressed them dramatically against her heart. "Handwritten by the one and only Rain Blackburn!"

"You showed them to me," Shanon said with a smile. "Twice."

"Did I hear my cousin's name?" asked Maxie Schloss, the fourth suitemate, as she entered the sitting room. Max had joined the suite just that year. Lisa McGreevy, one of the four original Foxes, had decided not to return to Alma.

"I was just showing Shanon the letters he sent me," said Palmer. She had met Rain at Max's Christmas party in New York. He was eighteen, rich, an incredibly talented musician, and had a smile that made Palmer's heart race. "It's really too bad that he lives in New York," she said wistfully.

"And that he already has more girlfriends than he can count," Max finished. "Don't get your hopes up."

"What's wrong with you?" Palmer asked in surprise. Max was almost always cheerful. She almost never heard her sound down about anything.

"Just a little interview with the *Brighton Observer*," Max said, slinging off her denim jacket. "Some brilliant reporter there made the absolutely earth-shaking discovery that I am Max Schloss's daughter."

"Oh, boy," said Shanon. If there was anything Maxie hated, it was someone trying to cash in on the celebrity of her famous father.

"This guy intercepted me on the way to history class. He's addicted to my father's TV show, and was wondering if it would be possible to do a story on the two of us. Naturally that would involve a meeting with my dad. It was so embarrassing—he was even quoting my father's jokes! I couldn't get rid of him, and of course, Mr. Seganish gave me a detention for being late to class. Which is where I've been up until now—copying genealogy charts of the Tudors. Who can keep them straight anyway? Everyone is named Henry!" She flopped down on the couch and put her head in her hands. "This isn't my day."

Shanon smiled at her roommate. "Maybe this will improve it," she said, pulling an envelope out of her pack. "You got mail today. In fact, you're the only one in the suite who did."

"Big deal," said Palmer. "I bet I'll get a letter from Sam tomorrow."

"I'm sure," Shanon agreed with a laugh. "Well," she said, holding the envelope out to Max, "aren't you going to open it?"

Maxie's face brightened. "Jose comes through again!" she said, referring to her nine-year-old pen pal.

"Not exactly," Shanon said.

Max's eyebrows rose in surprise as she took the envelope. The return address was Ardsley Academy. She was silent for a moment. "Paul Grant wrote to me," she said finally.

"You don't have to sound so stunned," Shanon said, grinning. "Weirder things have happened."

"Paul Grant?" Palmer looked every bit as amazed as Max sounded. "The one with the jade-green eyes? The one who looks like a model for a tanning salon commercial?"

"He does not!" Max said, blushing furiously.

"You've got to admit he's pretty terrific-looking," Shanon said.

"He's okay," Max mumbled, folding the letter in half and shoving it in the pocket of her teal-blue vest.

"Oh, no, you don't," Palmer sang out gleefully. "You know the rule. You have to read it aloud."

"I have to read it to the whole suite," Max protested, "and Amy's not here."

At that very moment the door to Amy and Palmer's room flew open, and Amy stuck her head out. "Can you guys keep it down?"

"Traitor," Maxie muttered.

"Amy, you've got to come out here," Shanon said. "Max has a letter from a new pen pal."

"Jose is my pen pal," Max said firmly.

Palmer waved a handful of her letters in the air. "There's nothing wrong with having more than one."

"Especially when the second one happens to be Paul Grant," Shanon added.

Amy's eyes lit with delight. "The gorgeous Paul Grant?"

"Not you, too," Maxie moaned. She looked at her suite-mates in despair. "You're all boy crazy."

"Definitely," said Palmer with a laugh. "Now read that letter!"

"Later," Max said, edging toward the room she shared with Shanon. "I've got . . . homework to do."

"Now that's an original excuse," said Amy.

Shanon watched her roommate with interest. "You really like him, don't you?"

"I do not!" Max insisted, turning an even deeper shade of red. "Unlike three other maniacs I could name, I'm just not interested in boys. And as for Paul Grant—if you really want to know, I can't stand him."

Palmer couldn't resist. She'd never seen Max so flustered. Besides, she was dying to know what Paul Grant had written. She stood up, deliberately gazing out the window.

"If you're not interested in boys, then you can't be too interested in what that letter says," she began. Then she spun about quickly, snatching the letter from Max's pocket. "But I am!"

"Give that back!" Max demanded. "It's personal."

"Personal, huh?" Palmer slid a polished fingernail beneath the flap and opened the envelope. "I thought you said you couldn't stand him. What do you care if it's personal or not?"

"I don't care," Max snapped, advancing on Palmer. "I just don't like other people opening my mail!"

"You'd have to read it aloud sooner or later, anyway," Palmer teased, holding the letter overhead.

"Then *I'll* read it," Max said furiously.

Caught up in the game, Palmer danced across the room with Paul Grant's letter. Max reached for the letter and once again Palmer tried to snatch it out of the way—and the letter ripped in half. Palmer's blue eyes widened. "Max, I didn't mean—"

"Just forget it," Max snapped. She grabbed the other half of Paul's letter from Palmer and took it over to the desk, where she carefully matched the torn halves and began taping them back together.

Amy shook her head. "How much tape are you going to put on that thing? You're being awfully careful with a letter you don't care about. I think you like Paul Grant."

"Maxie's got a boyfriend," Palmer chanted softly.

"Please read it to us, Maxie," Shanon pleaded.

"All right already!" Max said desperately. "Anything to shut you three up." Max's green eyes skimmed the letter. "Oh, good grief!" she moaned.

Amy snuck up beside her. "Come on, Schloss, give!"

10

Max sighed loudly and finally began reading aloud: " 'Dearest Maxine—' Maxine," she repeated numbly. "Doesn't he know I hate people calling me Maxine?"

"I'm sure he'd be happy to call you Max," Shanon predicted.

"And *dearest*," Max went on in dismay. "No one except my eighty-six-year-old aunt uses that word!"

"Picky, picky," said Palmer. "Just keep reading. From the beginning, please."

"Might as well get it over with," Amy said, grinning.

"I guess." Max winced and began again.

Dearest Maxine:
Ever since the Valentine's Day Dance I've thought of nothing but you. Every time I close my eyes I see you—hair like waves of fiery silk, eyes like emeralds. Maxine, you are the most gorgeous girl alive. If this sounds like I have a heavy crush on you, I do. And you're the only one who can tell me what to do about it.

Awaiting your reply,
Paul Grant

Amy was rocking with laughter. "Waves of fiery silk," she giggled. "That's *bad*—I've got to use it in one of my songs."

"I thought the letter was wonderful!" Palmer said. She looked admiringly at Maxie. "Paul is so romantic."

"Yuk!" said Max. "This is gross!"

"What *are* you going to do about it?" Shanon asked her roommate.

"I don't know." Max sighed and slipped the letter inside her history book. "It's the mushiest, gooeiest thing I've

11

ever read! I don't know if I should just throw it out or write one back that's worse. 'Dearest Paul,' " she began in a syrupy voice, " 'You are the sun in my eyes and the wind in my toes. . . .' "

"Max!" Palmer said in a horrified voice. "You can't do that. And you can't throw out that letter. He's awaiting your reply."

"Well, he can 'await' awhile longer," Max said. "I already told you. I have a pen pal, and his name is Jose." She glanced at her watch. "Omigosh, I was supposed to meet Muffin Talbot at the library fifteen minutes ago."

Shanon looked at Amy and Palmer, who were sitting on opposite sides of the room. She wasn't eager to be left alone with the two feuding roommates. "I'll come with you," she said.

"Me, too," Amy said quickly.

A few minutes later the three girls left. Palmer was alone in 3-D. Slowly, she began to collect the letters that were still spread out on the floor. She put the envelopes back in a drawer in her desk, and stood still for a moment thinking. There was one more letter she wanted. One that was addressed to Maxine Schloss. Palmer would never understand her suitemate. Max didn't recognize true love when she saw it. She was going to throw out the most romantic letter ever written! Palmer shrugged and returned to the sitting room. Without a second thought, she took Paul Grant's letter from Max's book, and slipped it inside her purse.

CHAPTER TWO

Max sat alone in her room, staring at a blank piece of paper and chewing on the end of her pen. It had been exactly twenty-two hours since she'd read Paul Grant's letter, and she still hadn't answered it. She hadn't even been able to bring herself to look at it again, which didn't really matter since every word was etched permanently into her memory.

She hadn't been completely honest with her suitemates. Paul Grant's letter *was* the mushiest, gooeiest thing she'd ever read. But it was also the most thrilling letter she'd ever received. Paul Grant, who was every bit as good-looking as her suitemates said, thought *she* was gorgeous. He had a heavy crush on her! Now what was she supposed to do? Play it cool and hard to get? Admit that ever since the Valentine's Day Dance she'd had a serious crush on him? Ask him to be a little less enthusiastic in his next letter? "Dear Paul," she mused aloud, "I like you a lot, too, but could you please ease up on the mush?"

Maxie's mind kept going back to the Valentine's Day Dance and the way Paul Grant looked at her. It wasn't just that Paul was totally adorable. When he smiled at her there was so much warmth in his eyes. It felt as if he'd always been her friend—even before they'd met. As if somehow Paul Grant had liked her from the day she was born.

She shook her head sharply. "Snap out of it, Max!" she chided herself. "Soon you'll actually believe you're the most gorgeous girl alive." Trying to return to earth, she read the letter that had arrived for her that day.

Dear Max,

It was really fun playing with you and Gracie the other day. Dan and Maggie are lucky she's their dog. I want a pet too, but I don't know what kind I should get. My first choice is a dog, but my foster parents say we can't have one. They say the trailer is too small. Lila and Becky want a bird, but Billy thinks insects are cool. I don't think insects are good pets because they're not so affecshunut. What do you think?

Your pen pal,
Jose

Max smiled as she read Jose's letter. She knew exactly how he felt—she wished she could have a dog of her own, too, especially one like Gracie. Gracie was the Jack Russell terrier that the girls who lived in Fox Hall had bought for Maggie Grayson and Dan Griffith, their two favorite teachers, who had gotten married last summer. Max had always loved animals, but Gracie was special. Max had spent hours playing with the little white dog. Recently, she'd even started taking her to obedience classes. She'd never known a dog who was so sweet and smart and eager to please. *Maybe*, she thought, *we can get Miss Pryn to* change the rules about students having pets and then Gracie could have puppies. . . . But in the meantime she had to think of something to write to her nine-year-old pen pal. What would be a good pet, she wondered, for four kids and two adults living in a trailer park? Suddenly Maxie knew what the perfect pet would be.

Dear Jose,

I've been thinking about your pet problem. I agree that insects are not too affectionate. And I always feel sorry for pet birds—it doesn't seem fair to keep them in cages when they're meant to have the whole sky. I know you want a dog, but it does sound like things are kind of crowded over there. What about a pet turtle? They don't take up much space or eat much food, and they don't need room to run. Plus they're really cute and fun to watch. Think about it, anyway. And in the meantime, if you're lonesome for a pet, you'll just have to come visit me and Gracie again.

Purrfectly yours,
Maxie

Max hummed to herself as she folded the letter and slid it into an envelope. Not only had she come up with the perfect pet for Jose, but she knew exactly how she was going to get it for him! She'd need to get a pass into town, but she was sure Maggie would help her with that. *Sometimes you're an absolute genius, Schloss*, she congratulated herself. She sealed the envelope, put a stamp on it, and was about to head for the mailbox when she realized that she still had another letter to write.

Maybe I'm not such a genius, she thought, sinking down

15

onto her bed. She didn't have the first clue about what she was going to say to Paul Grant.

Germaine Richards opened the door to her private room, one hand on her hip. Palmer took in the short, pale pink cashmere dress, the Italian pumps, and the diamond stud earrings twinkling beneath Germaine's sleek auburn hair. Palmer had grown up with money, as had most of her friends, but there was something about Germaine that was just so . . . naturally elegant. Even in jeans and a T-shirt, the older girl made the models in a Calvin Klein ad look shabby.

"Come in," Germaine said, waving a well-manicured hand. "Reid is already here."

Of course, Palmer thought. *When isn't Reid here?* The two upper-formers were practically glued together. As far as Palmer could tell, Reid Olivier worshiped Germaine Richards. In fact, she was progressing from being Germaine's devotee to her total clone. Recently, she'd even started wearing her hair like Germaine's, parted on the side and hanging in front, almost completely covering one eye. On Germaine, it looked mysterious; on Reid, it looked as if she had hair in her eyes. Palmer hid a smile as she remembered Amy saying, "Sometimes, I just want to go up to her and say: 'Reid, buy a hairband. Or a barrette. Anything. Just get that stuff out of your face!' "

"So," said Germaine, "where did you come from?"

"Booth Hall. *We've* got mail." Palmer sat down on the sculpted ivory rug and opened her pack. She'd just picked up a letter from Sam, and one letter each for Germaine and Reid. Her ad had obviously worked.

"Don't tell me," Germaine said in a drawl that made it

clear that the entire universe bored her. "We got more replies for that ad you placed in the Ardsley *Lion*."

"You mean you've already gotten some?" Palmer asked in surprise. "I just sent the ad in last week."

"The marvels of modern communication," Reid said, producing a handful of envelopes.

"That's fantastic!" Palmer said. "I can't believe you got answers so soon. I mean—" She stopped herself as she saw Germaine's eyes narrow. It was never a good idea to be too enthusiastic around Germaine. Palmer thought briefly of her own suitemates—letters from their pen pals were the highlight of the day. But she put the thought aside immediately. After all, Amy wasn't speaking to her, Max hadn't been too warm ever since she tore Paul Grant's letter, and Shanon's true love in life was obviously Latin.

"Listen to this," Reid said, picking up one of the letters. "You'll never believe it!"

Dear Reid,
You want a boy, you got one. I'm in my first year at Ardsley. I'm 5'3" with brown hair, brown eyes, and glasses—not exactly Mel Gibson but not bad, either. I'm into bird watching and I'm on the debating team. When I saw your ad in the Lion, *I thought maybe this year wouldn't be a total waste, after all. Please write and tell me about yourself.*

Sincerely,
Sheldon Springarn

"Sheldon Springarn," Reid repeated. "Sheldon Springarn!"

Germaine smiled. "Oh, he's not so bad," she said sar-

17

castically. "After all, he's all of five feet three and in his first year. And he's into bird watching. You want a boy—you got him!" Her smile vanished as her eyes met Palmer's. "Didn't the ad say we were only interested in upperclassmen?"

"Well, no," Palmer admitted, wondering how she could have left out that vital piece of information. "I guess I forgot."

Germaine gave a weary sigh and opened the letter Palmer had just brought in. "Let's see what today's Prince Charming has to say."

Dear Germaine,

> *Roses are red*
> *Violets are blue*
> *You wanted a pen pal*
> *So I'm writing to you*

Germaine groaned and Palmer felt her face turn red, as if somehow she was responsible for the awful poem. "Is that all it says?" she asked miserably.

"Oh, no, there's more," Germaine assured her, and continued reading:

Well, I guess you can see I'm no poet. My name is Lenny Callen and I'm 5'10" and will be fifteen in a couple of weeks. I play halfback on Ardsley's JV team, and it's been too long since I've had a babe (if you know what I mean). If you want a hot date, make sure you like football, comics, and pizza. And write back soon!

> *See ya around,*
> *Lenny C.*

Reid was laughing so hard Palmer thought she was going to fall off the bed. "Well," Reid said, gasping for breath, "we know why it's been so long since he's had a 'babe.' "

Germaine rolled her eyes. "Just what I was hoping for," she said, "a hot date with a junior varsity jock who's into comics and pizza."

"Want to swap for Sheldon?" Reid asked. "At least Lenny's not a midget."

Germaine yawned. "Tempting as the offer is, I think I'll pass." Her dark eyes lit briefly on Palmer. "I can't believe you waste your time writing to a bunch of turkeys. This pen pal stuff is the boringest idea of the century."

"Wait a minute," Palmer said. "You can't judge all pen pals by those letters."

"Why not?" asked Reid, brushing her hair away from her face. "The other letters we got were no better. I got one from Harry Someone who spent three pages telling me about his new aquarium."

"Patience, Reid," Palmer said. "Sooner or later you'll get a letter from someone who you just know is really great."

"Like who?" Germaine asked.

"Like Sam O'Leary," Palmer said. "You know, he *is* almost famous. He and The Fantasy were on TV. And he writes great letters."

"Oh, please," said Germaine, tossing her letters aside. "He's so juvenile and he goes to that awful public school in Brighton. He delivers pizzas! What could he possibly have to say that's so great?"

"I'll show you," Palmer said, her blue eyes flashing as she drew Sam's envelope out of her pack. For a moment she hesitated. After all, she was supposed to share the

19

letters from her pen pals with her suitemates. But it had been ages since she'd shared anything with Amy. . . .

"We're waiting," Reid said impatiently.

Palmer took a deep breath and read Sam's letter aloud.

Hey, Palmer—

How's my favorite Fox? You've been on my mind, girl. Last night I couldn't sleep. I wound up taking this crazy walk at one in the morning, and nearly walked to Alma! (If only Fox Hall had balconies . . . it could have been very Romeo and Juliet.*)*

Anyway, I got your letter about the B-52's concert. Palmer, I wish I could take you (I wish I could take me, *that band is so hot) but you know the situation: 75% of what I earn goes into a savings account for college. And the remaining 25% wouldn't even buy us B-52's T-shirts.*

But despair not, fair maiden. A bunch of my similarly broke friends have decided that we're not going to sit home and mourn on concert night. Instead, we'll be at Brighton Bowling Lanes, breaking all records. So why don't you see if you can get a pass and join me there? I can't keep wandering around in the middle of the night, pining away for you.

> *Yours and only yours,*
> *Sam*

P.S. At least one good thing came out of that walk—I wrote a song about you—but you'll have to see me if you want to hear it.

"Bowling?" Germaine's laughter snapped Palmer back to reality. "He can't afford the B-52's concert, and he expects you to go bowling instead. Is he serious?"

"Sounded that way," Reid said. "I certainly wouldn't be

caught dead with someone like that. I mean, really, Palmer, what have you got to look forward to with him? Now it's bowling. Next time it will be miniature golf, and before you know it you'll be doing something really sophisticated like tossing water balloons."

Palmer opened her mouth to defend Sam, but instead she found her eyes drawn back to the letter. This time when she read it her heart didn't race. This time, she had visions of herself and Sam playing miniature golf while Germaine and Reid waved to them from the back of a limo. He couldn't even afford to go to a concert, and he made it sound as if going bowling was the perfect substitute. His letter was almost embarrassing.

"I guess I'm just surprised," Reid went on. "I always thought you had decent taste."

Palmer prayed that the floor would open and swallow her.

"Look," Germaine said in a soothing tone, "it's obvious he's crazy about you, and that's flattering and all, but Sam simply comes from a different background. Sooner or later that's going to cause problems. This thing with the concert is just the beginning. For as long as you and Sam O'Leary are together, he'll never be able to give you what you need."

There was so much truth in what Germaine said that Palmer was silent for a moment. Would life with Sam be one disappointment after another?

Reid stood up and stretched. "Like we said, there's no point to this pen pals scheme."

"That's not true," Palmer insisted. "What about Rain Blackburn? I showed you his letters. Rain has plenty of charm *and* money."

"Rain Blackburn is in New York," Germaine pointed out. "I thought the point was to have a pen pal you could date."

"There isn't anyone cool at Ardsley," Reid declared.

Palmer decided there and then that if she did nothing else in her life, she would prove Reid Olivier wrong. "I happen to know someone who's available," she said. "John Adams."

"The guy who just dropped Amy Ho?" Reid asked.

"That doesn't make him desirable," Germaine said with a laugh. "Who wouldn't drop Amy Ho?"

Surprisingly, Palmer felt stung. Amy wasn't exactly her favorite person at the moment, but she was still her roommate.

"John Adams *is* good-looking," Reid said thoughtfully. "Maybe I'll take him—even though he's a bit young."

"Not until we see one of his letters first," Germaine said. "Let's make sure he's not another loser."

"No problem," Palmer said decisively. "He writes great letters, and Amy has tons of them. I'll borrow one from her."

"Good," said Germaine. She picked out a CD and slipped it in the player. Palmer didn't recognize the singer, but a woman's sultry voice filled the room. "So," Germaine continued thoughtfully, "you're writing to the sensational-but-distant Rain Blackburn and the sweet-but-poor Sam O'Leary. Amy got dumped by John Adams, and Shanon is writing to Mars Martinez. What about that oddball Max Schloss, the comedian's daughter?"

"Don't tell me *she* has a pen pal," Germaine said.

"Actually, she has two," Palmer said proudly. She told them about how Max wrote Jose and Paul. "In fact,"

Palmer went on, determined to impress the two older girls, "I have Paul's letter with me."

"Why are you carrying around *his* letter?" Reid asked.

Palmer blushed. She was embarrassed to admit she'd stolen it from Max. "I didn't think Max would mind. I wanted to have an example of a good letter to show you."

"Why didn't you say so earlier?" Reid demanded.

"Do you want to see it or not?" Palmer asked.

Germaine held out her hand, and Palmer gave her the letter, sure that this one would finally convince Germaine and Reid that pen pals were cool. "Well?" she asked as Germaine finished the letter and handed it to Reid without comment.

"It's totally corny," Germaine said. "Especially coming from Paul Grant."

"You know Paul Grant?" Palmer asked.

"Our families used to vacation together on Martha's Vineyard," Germaine said. "I haven't seen him for about five years, but I remember him, all right. He's chubby and has a nose that turns up just like a little pig's."

"It can't be the same Paul Grant," Palmer said. "The Paul Grant at Ardsley is gorgeous."

"Only if you like people with knobby knees," Germaine said. "I know it's the same Paul Grant. His parents decided to send him to Ardsley at the same time that mine enrolled me at Alma. I was always sure it was a conspiracy. Still, despite the fact that he looks like a baby pig, you're dumb if you don't snatch him from Max Schloss."

"Why?" Palmer asked. "You just finished telling me how gross he is."

"Well," Germaine said, "he's not my type, but the Grant family has major money. One day Paul Grant is going to own six estates, including a château in France, his own shipping line, and a giant automobile company."

Palmer's eyes widened. "That much money?"

"Maybe *I'll* be his pen pal," Reid piped up.

"I couldn't let you do that," Palmer said quickly. "I mean . . . Max might get upset."

"You mean *you* might get upset," Germaine said. "I don't know about Max, but I'd say you're the one who likes Paul."

Once again Palmer was forced to acknowledge that Germaine had an uncanny knack for seeing through people. "I'm—I'm mildly interested," Palmer hedged. "The problem is that I have two pen pals already and I don't have time to write another one."

"Dump one," Germaine suggested. "You already know it won't work out with Sam in the long run."

"I can't do that to Sam!" Palmer said indignantly. Even if Sam's letter had embarrassed her, they'd been through a lot together, and usually she loved getting his letters. And she certainly wouldn't dream of not writing to Rain Blackburn, especially since he'd just started writing to her! "Besides," Palmer went on, "even though Max says she doesn't like Paul, I think she does."

"Suit yourself," said Germaine. She looked at Palmer curiously. "Remember when you and your loyal suitemates used to call yourselves the Foxes of the Third Dimension? Do you still do that?"

"Kind of," Palmer admitted. "I mean, only sometimes."

"Don't you think it sounds a little . . . young?" Germaine asked.

Now that Palmer thought about it, it did sound young. Young and stupid.

"Really," Reid said. "Whoever heard of a person calling herself a fox just because she lives in Fox Hall?"

Palmer forced herself to smile. "We don't really say it that much anymore—" she began.

But Germaine wasn't listening. "Imagine," she said, "if you and Paul Grant become pen pals, you'll be a fox and a baby pig!"

Reid laughed as if this was the funniest thing she'd ever heard, and Palmer's smile grew even stiffer.

"Don't worry about it," Germaine said, dismissing the subject. She winked at Palmer. "I'm sure true love will find a way. Listen, you two, my mother called this morning and said that we'll be chartering a yacht for the month of July. Daddy wants to sail the Caribbean. She told me I could bring two friends, so why don't you check with your parents and see if your schedules are open?"

"I'm sure it's fine with my parents," Reid said instantly.

Palmer blinked. She'd just been invited for a month-long cruise with the Richardses! It was a world away from being invited to go bowling with Sam. *And those two worlds just don't mix*, Palmer told herself. The problem was she knew exactly which world she wanted to belong to. "I'll check with my parents," she told Germaine. Now she wouldn't have to go to California to share her father's attention with her stepsister, Georgette, during her summer vacation. The only other alternative was staying with her busy mother in Palm Beach. The more Palmer thought about it, the more she realized how lucky she was to have a friend like Germaine.

CHAPTER THREE

———◆———

"Way to go, Ho!" Shanon and Max cheered. "Go, Amy!"

With the score at three to two in the last inning, the team from Shady Lane Prep was in the lead. But at the last minute, Amy had just done the impossible—she'd brought in a victory for Alma!

"That's five straight wins," Shanon said, watching Amy surrounded by her teammates. "I think the catcher's in danger of being hugged to death by the rest of her team."

"This win means we're neck and neck with good old Brier Hall for the conference trophy," Max said as the final score was posted. "Why is it that every time Alma has a team that's winning, Brier Hall has one that's just as good?"

Shanon grinned. "What else are archrivals for?"

"They haven't got a chance," Max said confidently. "We've got softball's secret weapon—Amy Ho."

"Honestly," came Palmer's voice from behind them, "you'd think Amy was the only person on the team. She did have some help, you know."

Shanon turned around in surprise. "Where were you? We searched all over the bleachers."

Palmer shrugged and nodded toward the field. "I was sitting down there with Germaine and Reid. We came during the second inning. They left a few minutes ago."

"Oh," Shanon said, wondering why she felt hurt. After all, Palmer had a right to sit with whomever she wanted. Still, Shanon had hoped all of the Foxes would be there *together*, cheering Amy on. She knew that Amy and Palmer weren't getting along, but it felt as if Palmer had just snubbed all of 3-D.

"Did you see Amy win?" Max asked.

But before Palmer could reply, Shanon blurted out, "Why didn't you sit with us?"

"Yes, I saw Amy," Palmer said flatly, "and I didn't sit with you because you were too busy talking to notice me!"

"All you had to do was sit down beside us," Shanon said. "We would have noticed you."

Max eyed the brilliant pink top that Palmer wore over a short brilliant green skirt. "You *are* kind of hard to miss."

Palmer put her hands on her hips, a sure sign that she was about to give someone a hard time. "There's Maggie," Shanon said quickly, wanting to avoid an outburst.

The pretty young teacher waved at the three girls, her other arm resting lightly around her husband's waist.

"Good grief!" Palmer exclaimed. "She really looks pregnant."

"That's probably because she is," Max explained with exaggerated patience.

"Very funny!" Palmer said. "Just think. Next September there's going to be a little Grayson-Griffith in Fox Hall, up all night, screaming its little lungs out."

"Is that really how you think of it?" Shanon asked in surprise. Like most of the girls in Fox Hall, she'd been looking forward to the baby's arrival. She'd already asked Maggie and Dan if they'd let her baby-sit.

"You've got it all wrong, Palmer," Max said. "Babies are great. They're cute and sweet and they change every single day."

"You mean you have to change them every day," Palmer said.

"I think Maggie and Dan will take care of most of that," Shanon said soothingly. "Unless, of course, *you* volunteer to baby-sit."

Palmer looked alarmed, and Shanon laughed. "The real question is, what are we going to get Maggie and Dan for a baby gift? I'd like to get them something before school lets out—you know, just in case he or she arrives early."

Maxie closed her eyes, summoning divine inspiration. "I know!" she cried. "An Alma gym suit!"

"What?" Palmer and Shanon said together.

Max shrugged. "Everyone here gets one anyway. The baby might as well get a head start."

"I can tell this is going to take some discussion," Shanon said. "Why don't we round up Amy and come up with a few alternate ideas?" She grinned at Max. "Not that the Alma gym suit isn't a splendid idea—I'm sure every baby in the country is dreaming about one, but . . ."

"All right already!" Max said, grinning. She turned toward Palmer. "Are you coming with us to congratulate Amy?"

"No," said Palmer.

"Why not?" Shanon asked, dreading the answer.

Palmer checked her watch. "I've got better things to do than hang around a locker room, listening to everyone relive a softball game. I've got tennis practice." Without

28

looking back, she strode off toward the tennis courts.

"Geez," Max said. "Do you think she's mad?"

"Could be," Shanon said thoughtfully.

Max looked remorseful. "She's probably angry because I teased her about the baby."

"No," Shanon replied. "She was mad before that came up. It's Amy."

Max groaned. "Still?"

Shanon sighed. "Amy's been freezing her out. I think Palmer would actually like to be friends again, but Amy's still furious over losing Emmett. And the softball team's success just makes things worse."

"What has that got to do with anything?" Max asked as they approached the gym.

"The softball team's winning, and—"

"The tennis team is losing," Max finished.

"Every match they've played," Shanon agreed. "I've been covering all the school games for that article I'm doing for *The Ledger*. Palmer's pretty good, but everyone else is a disaster. I can't believe they have the courage to keep showing up. And Palmer's so competitive," she went on. "Amy winning all the time must really bug her."

"That's the dumbest thing I've ever heard," Max declared. "Both tennis and softball are Alma teams. Anyway, Amy's her *roommate*. Palmer should be happy to see her win."

Shanon sighed as they entered the locker room. "You know Palmer."

"I'm getting to know her more and more," Max grumbled.

Amy had showered and changed, and was stuffing her

uniform into her black leather pack when Max and Shanon caught up with her.

"Hey, champ," Maxie called over the noise of banging lockers, "you were dynamite!"

Shanon gave her a quick hug. "You won it, Ho!"

Amy blushed and pulled her long hair back into a ponytail. With her spiky bangs, it managed to look neat and punk all at once. "Yeah, we did all right," she said, smiling. She could still feel the warm glow of victory. She nodded toward the girl behind her. "Clea's hit in the first inning really helped. It feels so great to be on a team like this."

"Modesty will get you everywhere," Max teased, then ducked as Amy swatted her on the head with her red baseball cap.

"So where's the celebration?" Shanon asked.

Amy wrinkled her nose. "Someplace very exotic. We're going to cool out at the snack bar. You'll come along, won't you?"

"Wouldn't miss it," Max assured her.

But someone would, Amy realized. She looked at her two suitemates and knew she had to ask. It just felt too weird to pretend that nothing was wrong. "Where's Palmer?"

"Tennis practice," Max answered quickly.

"Do you—do you know if she was at the game?" Amy asked, careful to keep her voice neutral. She almost hated herself for asking. Why should it matter whether or not Palmer had seen the game?

"Palmer was sitting up front," Shanon said in her peace-making tone. "She thought you were great. She told us to say congratulations."

30

Amy raised one skeptical eyebrow. "Did she really?"

"Well . . ." Shanon hedged, "I'm sure she meant to say it."

"Right." Amy furiously zipped her pack closed. "Palmer hates me these days. There's no sense denying it."

"Do you hate her?" Max asked.

"Not really," Amy said matter-of-factly. "I just don't like her anymore." She walked out of the locker room without looking back.

Palmer streaked across the tennis court and slammed the ball against the wall. She was hot and sweaty and thirsty, but none of it mattered. In fact, practice didn't matter, because her partner, Jeannie Lawson, hadn't bothered to show up. Again. Which explained why Jeannie was such a lame player. She gave tennis about as much attention as Palmer gave Latin.

At least when I mess up in Latin, I'm the only one who suffers, Palmer thought angrily. *But Jeannie is messing up Alma's entire team. I've never met anyone so insensitive in my entire life! Except maybe for Amy Ho.*

Amy Ho. Why did her thoughts keep returning to Amy? *Because she's on that miraculous softball team,* Palmer answered herself as she missed the ball. *And because she's my roommate and she hates me.*

Palmer was sure that Shanon and Max were shutting her out, too. Max and Amy had become close ever since Christmas vacation when the two New Yorkers had hung out together. Maxie was definitely on Amy's side. And as for Shanon . . . even Palmer had to admit that Shanon tried not to take sides. But the truth was that Palmer felt she had less in common with Shanon than with any of the others.

Maybe it was because Shanon's family didn't have money, or because Shanon was such a total brain. In any case, it had gotten to the point where there was no one in 3-D Palmer could talk to.

After all we've been through, she fumed, beginning another furious volley against the wall. *At least there's Germaine*. Palmer caught the ball and stood still for a moment, struck by the idea. Was Germaine Richards actually her friend? It was a strange thought, considering how cutting Germaine could be. She'd never felt as comfortable with the older girl as she felt with the Foxes. But Germaine understood her and didn't hate her for being herself. After all, Germaine had invited her on a month-long cruise.

"Palmer! Oh, Palmer!" A high girlish voice cut through Palmer's thoughts.

"Oh, great," Palmer moaned, letting the racket slip from her hand. "Just what I need—little Suzy Sunshine."

"I was watching you," sang out her stepsister, Georgette. Georgette was wearing white shorts with a peach T-shirt. Although she was only about a year younger than Palmer, she was wearing her blond hair in pigtails and looked about eleven. "That wasn't bad," Georgette said with authority. "Your backhand's really coming along."

"How would you know?" Palmer asked irritably. "You don't play tennis."

"I've watched Dad play," Georgette said sweetly.

That was the main thing about Georgette that Palmer couldn't stand. Georgette had totally taken over her father. Since the divorce, Palmer's father had lived in California with Georgette and her mother, Alicia. Palmer had stayed with her mother in Florida. She only got to see her father on holidays and vacations. It killed Palmer that Georgette seemed to know more about her own father than she did.

Palmer decided to do the diplomatic thing. She would pretend that Georgette wasn't standing there. Maybe she could even pretend that Georgette had never been born. She lifted the racket and served against the wall.

Georgette frowned. "You need to put more power into it."

She didn't say that, Palmer told herself calmly. *Georgette is a figment of my imagination.*

"You know," Georgette continued, "you don't have to practice alone."

Without losing her rhythm, Palmer replied, "Oh, are you going to find Jeannie Lawson for me?" Georgette was too annoying to ignore.

"No, silly. You can ask Sam to play with you."

Palmer lost the ball for what seemed like the tenth time in the last five minutes. She whirled on her stepsister. "What do you mean, I can ask Sam to play with me?"

"He's been taking tennis lessons," Georgette said. "Didn't he tell you?"

"No, he—" Palmer stopped as she saw Georgette's blue eyes widen in dismay.

"I shouldn't have told you," Georgette groaned. "He probably wanted to surprise you and I blew it."

"Oh, it doesn't matter," Palmer snapped. The mention of Sam O'Leary brought back all the embarrassment she'd felt when she'd read his letter aloud to Germaine and Reid. Although he'd written her two more letters since then, she hadn't been able to bring herself to answer them. Not since he'd offered to take her bowling instead of to the concert. She would never live that one down.

Georgette grabbed Palmer's arm. "What do you mean it

33

doesn't matter? Sam O'Leary is one of the greatest guys in the entire state."

"Maybe," Palmer said, shaking her arm free. "But we haven't written to each other lately."

"Why not?"

"Because . . . because he's boring. His letters are all the same. School and rehearsing with his band, and now . . . going bowling with the guys. If you really want to know, I find Sam O'Leary juvenile!"

Georgette stepped back as if she'd been slapped. "I can't believe you're saying this."

"Look," Palmer said wearily, "it's really none of your business. This is between Sam and me. Why don't you go braid your pigtails or something?"

"But you were crazy about him."

"Things change," Palmer said.

Georgette backed away as if her stepsister had a contagious disease. Palmer watched her go, feeling nothing. All she knew was that less than two months ago she'd been one of the Foxes of 3-D. They'd all been friends. They'd had a lot of good times together. And her pulse had quickened every time she got a letter from an exceptionally nice, good-looking drummer named Sam O'Leary. Now the Foxes hated her, and she couldn't bear to hear from Sam. Things had definitely changed . . . but she wasn't sure if it was for the better.

CHAPTER FOUR

Palmer—

Are you all right? It's been a while since I've heard from you, and I'm starting to get worried. I'm having nightmares about you getting tired of New Hampshire and chartering a private jet to the Riviera or something.

Beautiful Brighton is about the same as it was last time I wrote. School is school. I got sentenced to a week's worth of running the track at 7 a.m. 'cause I cut gym. Maybe cutting gym wasn't such a great idea.

Things are looking up for The Fantasy. Believe it or not we got an agent! He saw us on TV and called and said he'd be able to get us gigs. So we agreed to a trial period, and he's already got us booked to do the background for some minor advertising video. It's just an instrumental, but they asked me to write a new piece of music for it. I've got to come up with something really hot.

Which isn't easy when my main source of inspiration isn't answering my letters. Just send a note telling me you're okay, so I don't worry about you. I miss you, girl.

Lonely but getting plenty of exercise,
Sam

Palmer had returned from the tennis courts to find Sam's letter on her pillow. One of the Foxes must have left it there for her. She'd opened it without interest. *Definitely juvenile and boring*, she told herself as she finished reading it. Even the news about The Fantasy seemed dull. What could really happen with some small-town rock band with a small-time agent? But Sam's first paragraph shook her. It was almost as if he knew what was going on. *Except that it's not New Hampshire I'm tired of,* she thought, *it's you.* She folded the letter neatly, put it back in its envelope, and deposited the whole thing in the wastepaper basket.

For what must have been the twentieth time, she unfolded Paul Grant's letter to Max. Max had never noticed that the letter was missing. In fact, she hadn't mentioned Paul's name since the day the letter arrived. Palmer couldn't figure it out. Paul was so cute and wrote such a sweet, romantic letter, *and* he was rich. What was wrong with Max? How could she *not* like him? Obviously, she didn't know a great guy when she saw him.

Palmer skimmed the letter again, her eyes resting on the words "awaiting your reply." The poor guy was probably still waiting. *Paul Grant, you deserve a pen pal who appreciates you*, Palmer thought. *Or at least someone who can help you out.*

"That's it!" Palmer said aloud. "I can help Paul Grant!" She'd write to Paul on Max's behalf, and give him a few tips about how to approach her suitemate. This way, she'd be helping Max and getting to know Paul at the same time.

Palmer curled up on her bed with a sheet of her favorite blue stationery. "Dear Paul," she began. "You don't know me very well, but I'm one of Max's suitemates, and I thought maybe you'd like a little help. . . ."

Palmer looked up as she heard a sharp knock on the door of the suite. *Who could that be?* she wondered. Putting Paul's letter aside, she went to the door and found Reid Olivier there, peering through a curtain of brown hair.

"Reid," Palmer said, surprised. "What's up?"

"I came to get the letters John Adams wrote to Amy," Reid said.

Palmer had practically forgotten all about them. Secretly she thought that both Reid and John Adams were dweebs who deserved each other. "Come on in," she said. "I'll get them for you."

Without hesitating, Palmer went into her room and opened the second drawer of Amy's desk. She knew that was where Amy kept all her pen pal mail. Amy had all of John Adams's letters tied together with a black silk ribbon. "Here," she said, handing the letters to Reid.

Reid grinned. "Germaine's going to want to see these. But she didn't say I couldn't peek first."

Do you have to get her permission for everything? Palmer wondered. The more she was around Reid, the weirder Reid seemed. As if, without Germaine, she didn't exist at all.

Reid chose a letter from the middle of the pile and began to read it aloud:

Dear Amy,

I really liked the lyrics for that song you wrote about the rain. It made me think of the way it feels on Cape Cod during a storm. (My family has a summer house there.) So here's the next part, or the start of a new song or whatever:

37

After the rain
Everything washed clean
Leaves scattered by the wind
Driftwood high on the sand
And a tiny, perfect shell
Just for you

> *Sincerely,*
> *Beachcomber John*

"Aeldaj," Palmer said, frowning.

"What?"

"John used to be into acrostics. He'd write Amy these poems, and then if you read down the first letters of each line, they'd spell another word. But this one just spells 'Aeldaj.' I guess it was written before he got into acrostics." She looked up at Reid. "Well, what do you think?"

Reid shrugged, trying to look unimpressed. "I guess he's okay," she said. "I wonder where on the Cape their summer house is."

"I forget," Palmer said, "but I think it's pretty classy."

"Let's read another one," Reid suggested. "Maybe he'll say."

She had just unfolded a second letter when Palmer heard the sound of the door to the suite opening, then someone entering the sitting room. She didn't have to look up to recognize Amy's footsteps.

"Quick," she hissed at Reid, "hide those!"

Reid peered up through her hair. "Why?"

It was too late. Amy walked into the room, and reached for her guitar. Then her eyes fell on the letters from John Adams.

Palmer felt her face turning bright red as she met Amy's

furious gaze.

"What are you doing with those?" Amy asked in an icy voice.

It was, Palmer realized, the first time in weeks Amy had spoken to her directly.

"Uh—I—I was just showing them to Reid as an example of pen pal letters," Palmer lied. "Is that okay?"

"No, it is not okay," Amy told her. "Those are my letters, and they're my private property. You have no right to show them to anyone. You don't even have the right to touch them!"

Palmer felt herself flush again. Amy was humiliating her in front of Reid! She could just imagine Reid telling Germaine all about it. Palmer took a deep breath, determined to rescue what little pride she had left. "Amy, this really isn't a big deal," she said in a voice that she hoped sounded bored. "You and John Adams were never that close. You can't expect me to believe that you care—"

Palmer's speech faltered. Amy was ignoring her. Her roommate stalked over to where Reid sat on Palmer's bed, and grabbed John Adams's letters from the older girl. Slowly and deliberately she retied them with the black silk ribbon.

When she looked up, her dark eyes seemed to cut right through Palmer. "Let's get one thing straight," she said. "If you ever touch anything that belongs to me again without my permission, I promise you you'll be sorry."

"I'm already sorry I'm your roommate!" Palmer snapped.

But there was no answer except the slam of the bedroom door. Amy, her letters, and her guitar were gone.

"Whew!" Reid said. "That was quite a little tantrum. I

thought you said she wasn't interested in John Adams anymore."

"She's not," Palmer assured her. "The only one she's interested in is that dropout, creepo Emmett."

"In that case. . . ." Reid pushed a shock of frizzy brown hair out of her eyes. "Maybe I *will* write John Adams."

"Great," said Palmer, losing patience with Reid. "I've got a letter of my own to work on." She returned to her letter to Paul Grant, hoping the older girl would take the hint and leave.

Reid did not take the hint. "Writing to Sam?" she drawled. "Planning another hot bowling date?"

"If you must know," Palmer replied, "I'm writing to Paul Grant."

Reid looked delighted. "You're stealing him from Max!"

"I am *not!*" Palmer said indignantly. "I'm helping him. After all, Max isn't your average Alma student, and I don't think he had the right approach last time. I'm just going to write and offer to give him some free advice."

"You really want Paul and Max to get together?"

"Of course not," Palmer replied, "but it's a good excuse for writing to Paul myself. I just hope he answers me."

Reid shook her head. "I still don't see why you're bothering. Germaine says Paul looks like a baby pig."

Palmer's patience had reached its limit. "Reid," she said, "I know this is a revolutionary concept for you, but much as I like Germaine, I don't always agree with her. Sometimes the great Germaine Richards is wrong. "So you can go back and tell Germaine that I've seen Paul Grant, and he doesn't look anything like a pig!"

Shanon settled herself beneath one of the maple trees on the grassy quad, and started a letter to Lisa. Shanon and Lisa had been roommates until Lisa's parents separated. Lisa felt that her mother needed her now that her parents were living apart, so she'd returned to her home in Pennsylvania. Shanon knew that leaving Alma was hard on Lisa, especially because Lisa had fallen in love with her pen pal, Ardsley student Rob Williams.

Dear Lisa,

Yesterday Palmer and Amy had the big blowup. I don't know what it was about, since they both refuse to discuss it. All I know is that they've both stopped speaking through me. This means they're not speaking at all, but honestly, it's kind of a relief. I hated being in the middle of it.

Even Mars is nearly incommunicado. He got a bad case of the flu and wound up in the infirmary. According to Rob (you knew I'd bring him up, didn't you?), he spends most of his days sleeping or trying to irritate the nurses. His last letter to me was basically an in-depth comparison of cough medicines. Poor boy. I think the flu went to his brain. He must be driving the rest of the Unknowns crazy.

How are things on the home front? I keep hoping you'll write and tell me that you'll be back at Alma in the fall. But whatever you decide, keep writing. I need to hear from someone sane!

Love,
Shanon

CHAPTER FIVE

Max read the page on Henry VIII for the eighth time, and realized she hadn't absorbed a word of it. Her forehead sank to the library desk.

"Miss Schloss?" inquired a crisp voice. "Is there a problem?"

Max turned her head and focused one eye on the librarian. "No, Ms. Jones, nothing's wrong."

"Then I'll thank you to sit up. The Alma Stephens library is not the place for napping."

"Yes, Ms. Jones." Max sat up, and her eyes returned to her history text. *This is completely useless*, she thought. *Today's Saturday and I've got a test on Monday and I can't concentrate.* Actually, the problem was she couldn't concentrate on history. There was definitely something she was concentrating on: the letter she still hadn't written to Paul Grant. *If I don't answer him soon, school is going to be over*, she realized.

"Studying for history?" Shanon whispered, taking a seat beside Max.

"Not exactly," Max confessed. "But I'm trying."

"Divorced, beheaded, died, divorced, beheaded, survived," Shanon quoted mysteriously.

"What?"

"That's how you remember what happened to Henry VIII's wives." Shanon frowned. "Or something like that. I might have gotten the order mixed up."

Max grinned. "Thanks a lot. You're a big help."

"Anytime." Shanon opened one of her books and began reading. After a few minutes she looked up. "Actually," she said, "I was looking for you because I wanted to ask for your help."

"What's up?" Max asked.

"I've been thinking. We've got to do something to get Amy and Palmer back together. It's been days since either of them has admitted that the other one is alive."

Max shook her head. "I don't like what's going on any better than you do, but I'm not sure this is our call. I think Amy and Palmer have to work this one out on their own."

"But they're not," Shanon said. "They just avoid each other. Palmer hangs out with Germaine and Reid, and Amy lives, breathes, and dreams softball."

A grin tugged at the corners of Maxie's mouth. "At least the softball team is getting something out of this."

"Maybe if we all did some fun things together, they'd make up," Shanon suggested.

"Fun things?" Max echoed. "It seems like a long time since any of us did anything that was fun."

"Exactly!" Shanon said.

Standing behind the library desk, Ms. Jones peered at them over her glasses. "Miss Davis, may I remind you that this is a library?"

43

"Sorry," Shanon whispered. She turned back to Max. "Well, what do you think of my plan?"

Max was about to make a wisecrack, when she realized there *was* something they could do all together. "You know," she said, "when I get done with the house of Tudor here, I'm going to Maggie and Dan's to ask for a pass into town later this afternoon. Jose's been dying for a pet, and I thought I'd buy him a turtle. We could all go and pick it out together. Then we could stop at Figaro's for pizza and see if Sam is working." She grinned. "That ought to convince Palmer to come."

Shanon smiled. "Sometimes I can't believe Palmer got lucky enough to hook up with someone as nice as Sam."

"It doesn't take much luck," Max said with a sigh. "Palmer's gorgeous, and she knows it. Every boy wants to go out with her."

Shanon studied her roommate's face, and hesitated a moment. "Well," she said softly, "at least one boy we know of thinks you're gorgeous and wants to go out with you."

Max buried her head in her arms with a moan.

"Miss Schloss," said the ever-vigilant Ms. Jones.

"I know, I know." Max forced herself to sit up.

Shanon gently touched Max on the arm. "I'm sorry. I shouldn't have said anything. It's none of my bus—"

Max sighed. "I may go crazy if I don't talk to someone about it." Ms. Jones cleared her throat loudly. Max rolled her eyes, sending Shanon into a fit of giggles. "Maybe we should go somewhere else to discuss this. After all, this *is* a library."

"You've got to swear that you won't say anything to

anyone," Max said, taking one last slurp from her ice-cream soda. She and Shanon had been sitting in the Tuck Shop for twenty minutes, and it was only now that she'd gotten up the courage to talk about *him*.

"I swear," Shanon said. For a moment she thought guiltily about the letter she'd already sent Lisa. Well, she wouldn't say anything from now on.

"Cross your heart and hope to die?"

"Max!"

"All right. I—I really like Paul Grant," Max began. "At least I think I do. I mean, I've only met him twice, and once I was dressed in a clown suit, so that time sort of doesn't count." She sighed, feeling her face turn as red as her hair. "It's not like we have a hot romance going or anything . . . which is why it was so weird getting that total mush letter. I've been thinking about him every single day since the Valentine's Day Dance, and somehow I never thought that when he wrote to me it would sound like *that*. It's . . . a little overwhelming."

Shanon tried to keep from smiling. "Does that mean you don't want him for a pen pal?"

"No!" Max said. The spoon she'd been holding slipped out of her hand and fell to the floor.

"Okay, okay." Shanon laughed as Max bent down to retrieve the spoon. "So," she said as Max sat up again, "you *do* want Paul for a pen pal. Just write him a letter. What's the problem?"

Max shut her eyes. "I don't know how."

"Of course you do. You write great letters to Jose," Shanon pointed out. "I know! Let's look at Paul's letter. You might get some ideas about what to write."

Max threw up her hands in exasperation. "You won't

believe this, but I can't find it anywhere! It must have fallen out of my history book." Max gave Shanon a woeful look. "You don't have this problem with Mars, do you?"

"When Mars and I started writing we were just pen pals," Shanon said. "It was totally casual. I had no idea we were going to start really liking each other. By the time we did, we were pretty comfortable together."

"That's what I wanted it to be like with Paul," Max said sadly. "I thought we could write and just get to know each other and—"

"You still can," Shanon said. "Just write him a normal letter. Maybe then he'll write back a normal letter."

"I guess," Max said, sounding unconvinced. She stirred her ice-cream soda.

"Max"—Shanon's voice was gentle—"what is it? It's not just the mushy letter that's bothering you."

Max shut her eyes again. "First time," she said so softly that Shanon barely heard her.

"First time what?"

Max opened her eyes, and said woefully, "It's the first time I've ever been 'in like.' "

Max knocked on Maggie and Dan's door and turned to Shanon. "Do you think Maggie will give us passes for the entire suite?"

"Sure she will—unless Palmer's got herself on warning again."

"I don't think so," Max said. "She actually got a C on the last Latin quiz."

Maggie opened the door, smiling. She was wearing a flowered-print maternity dress, and had her hair swept up in a twist. Gracie trotted up at once, her little tail wagging madly.

"Hi." Maggie looked down at the puppy. "I think she's as glad to have company as I am."

Max knelt to pet Gracie, and the puppy jumped up and licked her face.

"Gracie, let them in," Maggie said, laughing. "It's very rude to keep your visitors in the doorway."

Shanon and Max followed Maggie into the living room and sat down on the comfortable couch.

"How about some juice?" Maggie offered. "I've got apple and orange."

"Apple for me, please," Shanon said.

"And me," Max added. "Come here, Gracie," she said as Maggie went into the kitchen. "Let's show Shanon what a brilliant puppy you are. Just watch this," she told her roommate. "Gracie, sit," she commanded, giving the hand signal she'd learned in obedience class.

At once the little dog sat on her haunches, watching Max expectantly.

"Stay," Max said. Gracie remained where she was. "Now come," Max said. The terrier walked over to her, her tail wagging. "Sit," Max said again. Gracie sat again. "All done!" Max told the dog, petting her. "What a good girl!"

"You're having more success with her than Dan," Maggie said, coming into the room, holding a tray with three glasses of apple juice. "Last night Dan told her to sit, and she ran off to fetch her ball."

Shanon took a glass of juice. "Maybe she thought he said play," she suggested.

47

"Who knows," Maggie said, "but there was definitely some confusion there. So . . . did you two stop by just to see Gracie?"

"We wanted to get passes into town," Shanon explained. "For all of 3-D."

"We're going to buy Jose a turtle," Max added. "He wants a dog of his own, but the trailer's kind of crowded, so I thought a turtle would be just right."

"It's a sweet idea," Maggie agreed. "And you all want to go into Brighton?"

"We're not sure about Palmer and Amy," Shanon said. "We haven't asked them yet, but we'd like to."

"Just drop by before you leave and let me know," Maggie said.

While Maggie wrote out the passes Max played a serious game of hide-and-seek with Gracie. She pulled out one of the sofa cushions and crouched behind it. Gracie sniffed around the edges of the cushion, sure that her friend was close by.

"I'm going to tell her where you are," Shanon threatened.

"Don't you dare!"

"Time-out!" Maggie called, holding out the passes.

Max reached for her pass, and Gracie scooted around the cushion, launching herself into Max's lap with a joyous yip.

"She really loves you," Maggie said thoughtfully.

"It's completely mutual," Shanon assured the young French teacher. "I have a feeling Jose isn't the only one who wants a pet."

Max dropped a kiss on top of the puppy's head and

looked up. "Do you think Gracie could come into town with us this afternoon?" she asked impulsively.

Maggie looked doubtful. "I don't know—"

"She could ride in my bicycle basket," Max went on. "And then when we got into town, I'd keep her on her leash. She always does just what I ask. It won't be a problem. Honest."

"Dan does take her around on his bike," Maggie agreed, a hint of concern in her voice. She gave the two girls a long, thoughtful look, then smiled. "Since you've been so responsible with her . . ."

"You mean it?" Max cried, her face lighting up. "This is great! We'll go round up Amy and Palmer and then we'll come back in about an hour to pick up Gracie." Max couldn't stop smiling. Without meaning to, her gaze went to Maggie's round stomach.

"The baby's coming along, isn't she?" Maggie said, patting her stomach with a chuckle. "Here," she said gently, "you can feel her."

Timidly, Max put her hand out. "Wow . . . it's moving!" she said in amazement.

"Kicking is more like it," Maggie told her with a laugh. "When you come back to school next year, she'll be born— the youngest student at Alma."

"What if she's a he?" Shanon asked.

Maggie shrugged. "I guess Dan and I will have to transfer to Ardsley."

"You can't!" both girls said at once.

Maggie winked at them. "Relax, I don't think we'll have to worry about that for a while. Go ahead, find Amy and Palmer. I'll get Gracie ready for her trip into town."

CHAPTER SIX

It didn't take Max and Shanon long to find Amy. She was on her way out of Fox Hall, a pile of books in her arms.

"Looks like someone's headed for the library," Shanon said.

"Only for as long as it takes to return these," Amy told them. "I'm not going to let Ms. Jones ruin a perfectly good Saturday."

"A woman after my own heart," Max said solemnly. "What do you say to a ride into Brighton? We've already got you a pass from Maggie."

Amy laughed. "Do I have a choice?"

"Not really," Shanon assured her, "we've got your entire life planned out."

"Meet us at 3-D in about forty-five minutes," Max said.

"Right, coach!"

"Now," said Max as soon as Amy was safely out of earshot, "all we have to do is find Palmer."

Shanon's hazel eyes widened. "I almost forgot. I'm supposed to drop my article off at *The Ledger*. I'll look for Palmer on the way."

"And I will search ye halls of Fox, near and far, high and low, hither and yon," Max vowed in her most theatrical voice.

Shanon rolled her eyes. "Don't get lost. See you back at the suite."

"Anyone here?" Max called out as she let herself into 3-D.

There was no answer, which wasn't really surprising. She'd checked the common room, the kitchen, and even Germaine's room and had found no sign of Palmer in the dorm. *She's probably on the tennis courts*, Max told herself. She decided to check Palmer's room anyway. She knocked and when there was no answer, walked in.

Amy and Palmer's room was in its usual state. Neither one of the roommates was the neatest person in the world, but they were messy in different ways. Amy's walls were covered with posters of rock stars. Her guitar case lay open on her bed, sheets of music strewn around it. The top of her dresser was covered with her hat collection. Amy had at least a dozen hats, and some of them were pretty radical.

Except for a couple of tennis rackets, every surface on Palmer's side of the room was covered with a layer of scattered clothing and cosmetics.

Max shook her head, thanking her lucky stars for the umpteenth time that she'd gotten neat, considerate Shanon for a roommate. As she turned to leave the room, she saw something familiar on top of Palmer's desk. *It can't be*, she thought. But it was. Lying on top of one of Palmer's scarves was *her* letter from Paul Grant, taped up the middle.

What is she doing with it? Max wondered. *She probably found it lying around somewhere and forgot to give it back to me*. It didn't really matter why Palmer had the letter, Max decided. What mattered was that she stop procrastinating and write back to Paul.

Then she saw something else. Piled on the chair next to Palmer's desk were a bunch of questionnaires. Max thought for a moment about whether or not she should snoop. Then she decided that since Palmer had her letter, it was fair play.

The questionnaires had been sent by the Foxes to their pen pals the year before. They asked things like, "What's your favorite color? Favorite actress? Favorite vegetable? Favorite sport? If you were an animal, which animal would you be?" Max laughed as she read some of the answers. Maybe she should make up a questionnaire just like it for Paul Grant. Or at least ask him a few interesting questions.

Determined to get the job done, Max went into her own room, kicked off her sneakers, and curled up on her bed with a pen and her stationery. Her great-aunt had given her the stationery as a gift, and at the time Max had thought it was kind of fussy-looking. But now the ivory paper edged in green and gold trim seemed pretty and feminine. Paul would like it, Max thought. "Dear Paul," she began. And stopped. Maybe she should have started with "Hi, Paul," or just "Paul." She looked at his letter again, saw "Dearest Maxine," and decided that "Dear Paul" was fine. Now what? Should she thank him for his letter or would that sound too polite, like she'd taken etiquette classes or something? Maybe she should start by asking him some questions. Or should she tell him something about herself first? "Arrrgghh!" she groaned. "I hate this!"

"Hate what?" asked Shanon, sticking her head into the room.

"When did you come in?" Max asked.

"A few minutes ago. What do you hate?"

"Trying to write to Paul Grant," Max said glumly.

"Well, you're off the hook for now," Shanon told her. "We've got a dog to take into town, remember?"

Max felt a rush of pure relief. "Thank goodness." She hurriedly put away her stationery, and slipped on a lightweight jacket. "Any luck finding Palmer?"

"Nope, but Amy just came in."

"And she'd like to know *why* you got her a pass into town," Amy said. "What's going on?"

Max grinned and slung an arm around Amy's shoulder. "I know you'd never guess, so I'm going to give it to you straight: We're going to buy a turtle."

The three Foxes stood in the Brighton Pet Shop, gazing intently at the selection of turtles.

"I kind of like the little guy on the left," Shanon said. "He moves the fastest."

"You mean he moves," Amy said. "I don't think the word 'fast' applies to turtles."

"I think the guy on the rock has character," Max said.

"The one who keeps climbing on top of all the other turtles?" Shanon asked. "He's got an ego problem."

"Turtles don't have ego problems," Max said with great certainty.

"This one does," Shanon retorted.

Twenty minutes later the three friends had settled on a turtle. "Jose's going to love him . . . or her," Max said.

"When will you see Jose?" Amy asked.

Max frowned. "Not for another two weeks. They're repainting the town library, so they canceled this week's tutoring session."

"What are you going to do with a turtle for two weeks?" Shanon asked. "You know the dorm rule about no pets. If one of the dorm monitors finds out about our little guest . . ."

Max's expression became very innocent. "I don't see why we can't just keep him in the bathtub."

"Because it's impossible to keep anything a secret in Fox Hall," Amy replied. "Besides, can you imagine Palmer sharing the tub with a turtle? We need a Plan B."

"Right," said Max. She went to the front of the store and spoke with the woman who worked behind the register. "I've got it all worked out," she reported a minute later. "I'm going to put a deposit down on the turtle, and they'll keep it here for me until I'm ready to pick it up." She turned back to the tankful of turtles. "Now which one did we choose?"

The three girls came out of the pet store to find Gracie waiting patiently, her leash tied to a lamppost. "Good girl," Max said, kneeling to untie her. "Are you ready to go to Figaro's?"

The little white dog licked Maxie's face as she lifted her into the bicycle basket.

The route from the pet store to Figaro's skirted the outside of the town of Brighton. The girls rode down tree-lined streets, past white clapboard houses. It was a beautiful spring day. Flowers were in bloom, and the trees and grass were a bright shade of green. Everything seemed fresh and clean in the afternoon sun.

Amy was riding in the lead when she suddenly hit the brakes. Max and Shanon came up short behind her.

"What is it?" Max asked.

Amy nodded to a poster in the window of the local record store. It advertised Emmett and the Heartbreak, playing at a local club. Amy swallowed hard. She was still trying to forget Emmett. Even though her suitemates all thought he was a creep, Amy had seen a different side of him. She knew he was a gifted musician. The amazing thing was that he'd believed in her talent, too. He'd wanted her to sing lead in his band, and if it hadn't been for Palmer interfering, she'd be singing at this club. Well . . . maybe not. Technically, she was too young to sing in clubs. But that wasn't what hurt. What she couldn't deal with was that she'd had a chance to sing with a real rock band—and Palmer Durand had taken it away from her.

"Amy," Shanon said, "are you all right?"

Amy was still staring at the poster. "Fine," she said. She looked at it for a long moment, then took a deep breath. "Let's go."

Shanon drew her bike even with Amy's. "It still bothers you, doesn't it?"

"Very good, Holmes," Amy said, her voice cool. A second later she turned to Shanon and said, "I'm sorry. I didn't mean that. It's not your fault."

"You're still blaming Palmer, then."

"Who else should I blame? She's the one who wrecked everything."

Shanon was quiet for a while, putting all her energy into

55

pedaling. Amy was hard to keep up with. Maxie trailed a ways behind them, riding more slowly because of Gracie. When they finally reached a downhill stretch and began coasting, Shanon tried again. "I know Palmer had no right to interfere, but for once she was doing something that wasn't completely selfish. She was worried about you, Amy. We all were. We thought you were making a mistake. We were afraid Emmett would hurt you."

"It should have been my mistake to make," Amy said. "Palmer took away my chance."

"But in the long run she might have done you a favor."

Amy stopped her bike when they reached Figaro's and began to chain it to the bike rack. "It's like this," she said firmly. "For me freedom is being able to make your own choices every minute of the day. What you wear, what you do, who you spend time with. And whenever someone takes away my right to make a choice, they're not doing me a favor."

Shanon tried for the last time. "Emmett stole one of your songs."

"I know," Amy said softly. "But I still think I should have been allowed to deal with it on my own."

Maxie rode up to join them, breathing hard. "What was that?" she asked. "A race?"

"Just working out with Amy," Shanon said wearily. She smiled and reached out to scratch the puppy on the nose. "How did you like your bike ride?"

"She loved it," Max reported. "She looked so cute when we were coming down that hill. Her little ears were bent back in the wind." Max set the dog on the ground and snapped on her leash. "And now . . . it's time to pig out on pizza!"

Suddenly Sam O'Leary stumbled out of Figaro's, carrying a huge stack of pizza boxes. They could just barely see his wide-set gray eyes peering over the top box.

"Looks like the boy needs help," Amy teased.

Shanon grinned. "Maybe we should take a few of those pizzas off his hands."

"Are any of them Monstro sausage-mushroom?" Max inquired politely.

Sam grunted, staggered to the Za-wagon, set down his boxes, and turned to the girls. "I thought I recognized those voices," he said, smiling. His smile faded as he realized that Palmer wasn't with them. "Where's your roommate?" he asked Amy.

Shanon answered quickly. "We don't know. We looked all over for her, but she wasn't around."

"She's not sick or anything?" he asked, concerned.

"Only in her head," Amy muttered.

Sam gave Amy a sharp look, but all he said was, "She hasn't written to me for weeks."

"What?" Amy said. "All she's been into lately is pen pals. I even found her with—"

Amy never got to finish her sentence. There was a loud growl, and then a hard jerk on the leash that Max was holding. The next thing they knew Gracie was streaking down the street, a large Doberman in pursuit. "Gracie, come back!" Max shouted, taking off after the dogs.

"Oh, no," Shanon moaned, "we can't lose Gracie."

Sam hesitated for only a moment. "I may get fired for this, but get into the wagon. We'll see if we can catch them."

CHAPTER SEVEN

"This is like a bad cop show," Amy observed from the front seat of the Za-wagon, where she was wedged between Sam and the driver, Jason Reed. "Four young heroes, zooming through downtown Brighton in hot pursuit of a small terrier, a larger Doberman, and a missing Schloss."

"In a pizza delivery truck," Sam reminded her, winking at his friend Jason. "Don't forget who the real heroes are here."

"This isn't funny, you guys," Shanon said from the back. She was pressed against one wall of the truck, trying very hard not to fall onto the pizza boxes every time Jason turned a corner.

"We know," Sam and Jason said together.

"What happens if your boss finds out?" Amy asked.

"I'm sorry, Sam," Shanon said at once. "We don't want you to get in trouble. Maybe you'd better let us out now."

"Isn't that the Doberman?" Sam asked with a sharp nod to the right. A large black and tan dog was loping along the sidewalk, moving at a swift, easy pace.

"Sure looks like it," Amy said. "And it looks like the chase is over. Where are Max and Gracie?"

Jason turned a corner, and Sam said, "There's Max!" Max stood halfway down the block, her shoulders slumped and her head hanging. They pulled up beside her. "Max—you okay?" Sam called.

Max looked up slowly. Her face was streaked with tears. "I lost her," she sobbed. "I lost Gracie. Maggie trusted me and I lost Gracie."

Instantly Amy and Shanon were out of the truck, their arms around their friend. "It's all right," Shanon murmured. "We'll find her. I promise."

Max dried her tears, but she looked exhausted and miserable. "We—we better start searching," she sniffed.

Sam checked his watch and shot a questioning look at Jason. "We can give you about ten more minutes in the wagon," he offered. "Or we'll drive you back to your bikes if you want."

"That's okay," Shanon said, "we'll be fine."

Sam grinned. "Yeah, but I won't. I'll be worrying about you. Get in."

For the next ten minutes they cruised the streets of Brighton, searching for the small white terrier. At last the boys dropped them off by their bicycles.

"Thanks for your help," Max said.

"No problem," Sam said with a shrug. "I hope you find her. I'll keep my eye out when I make my deliveries. Say hi to Palmer for me, will you?"

"We will," Shanon promised as the two boys drove off.

"So," Max said, her voice still shaky, "what do we do now?"

"We keep searching," Amy said. "I think we should split up and meet back on campus."

"Sounds good to me," said Shanon. "See you two later—and good luck!"

Max was the last one to return to the campus. She found Shanon and Amy camped out under a maple tree on the edge of the quad.

"No luck, huh?" Amy said, reading Maxie's face.

Max shook her head as she got off her bicycle. "This has got to be the worst day of my entire life. . . . What are you guys doing out here?"

"We didn't want to go into the dorm," Shanon answered. "We weren't quite ready to meet up with Maggie or Dan."

"I know," Max said. "That's all I've thought about—how I'm going to tell them."

"Tell them what?" Palmer asked brightly, coming up behind them and plopping herself down on the grass.

Amy glared, and Max moaned and put her head in her hands. Shanon filled Palmer in on what happened.

For once Palmer was silent. At last she said, "Maggie and Dan have to be told."

"No kidding," Max said.

"But you don't have to do it alone," Palmer went on. "We'll all go with you."

Max looked up in surprise.

"I didn't think you even liked dogs," Amy said.

Palmer shrugged. "I don't, but Gracie's special." She looked straight at Amy. "When there's trouble the Foxes of 3-D stick together!"

Max stood stiffly, waiting for Maggie or Dan to answer her knock. Her heart was pounding and her stomach hurt. She couldn't remember ever having felt worse in her life.

Dan Griffith opened the door, his expression of welcome quickly changing to one of concern as he took in the faces of his visitors. "Come on in," he said. "Have a seat."

The four girls filed in and sat on the couch in a straight, solemn row.

"Is Maggie around?" Shanon spoke up. "Maybe you'd better get her."

Dan nodded. "Be right back."

It seemed to take forever before Dan and Maggie entered the living room. Maggie took one look at the girls and said at once, "It's Gracie, isn't it?"

Max nodded, trying not to cry. "I'm so sorry," she said in a broken voice.

"Oh, Maxie." Maggie knelt in front of Max and took her in her arms, holding her while she cried as if she'd never stop. "Now," she said when Max's tears finally subsided, "can you tell us what happened?"

Max nodded and, with the help of Amy and Shanon, told the sad story. Dan and Maggie listened quietly.

"You know, it's not hopeless," Dan said when she was done. "As far as we know, Gracie's still alive and healthy."

"And we're going to find her," Palmer said unexpectedly. "We're going to make posters and put them up all over town, and we're going to run ads in the newspapers, and we're going to alert all the animal shelters and veterinarians."

"We are?" Max asked in amazement. She'd been too upset to think that far ahead.

"Of course," said Palmer. "And we can ask Mars and

John to check on the Ardsley campus. You watch, we'll find this dog."

Maggie smiled a little sadly. "There's also a chance that someone might find her first, and won't want to give her back."

Max's lower lip began to tremble again.

"However," Maggie said quickly, "I think your ideas are good ones. They're certainly worth trying."

"Plus we'll keep searching," Dan said. He looked at his wife. "What do you say we take a drive into Brighton right now?"

Maggie nodded. "I'll get my sweater."

The girls stood up to leave.

"Hey," said Dan gently, "there's one more thing we have to get straight. This isn't your fault. The same thing could have happened to me or Maggie. If you want to blame anyone, blame the Doberman and its crazy owner who let it run loose." His hand rested on Max's shoulder. "Don't worry. We'll find her . . . somehow."

That night the sitting room of Suite 3-D was a flurry of activity. Using one of Max's photos of Gracie, Amy was designing posters; Palmer was writing ads for the local papers; Shanon was making a list of the Brighton animal shelters and vets; and a still-frantic Max was trying to help everybody do everything all at once.

"Max," Palmer said, "you're going to go crazy—or drive us crazy—if you keep this up. I think you need to sleep."

"I'm never going to sleep again," Max declared. "At least not till Gracie's found."

Shanon looked at Amy. "Should we tell her how ridiculous that is?"

"No," Amy said. "She'll figure it out." She frowned at the poster in front of her. "Could someone hand me a straightedge?" she asked without looking up. Palmer went into their room, got Amy's ruler, and gave it to her. "Thanks," Amy said, sounding surprised.

"You're welcome," Palmer said politely.

Shanon held her breath. Was this actually a truce?

But Palmer went back to her ads and Amy kept working on the posters.

Max darted around the room, unable to do much of anything besides worry. "I know what I can do!" she said at last.

Her three suitemates looked up at her.

"I can make a list of possible presents for Dan and Maggie's baby."

"Right now?" Shanon asked.

Max shrugged. "It'll take my mind off Gracie."

"Then do it," Amy said.

"Okay." Max got a big drawing pad, flipped to a blank sheet, and settled herself in the middle of the sitting room. "Let's hear some suggestions."

"When I was born, my aunt gave me a rattle made of sterling silver and mother-of-pearl," Palmer said. "It's so pretty. My mother still has it. Maybe we should get something like that."

Amy rolled her eyes but didn't comment.

"We could always get baby clothes," Shanon said.

"Or one of those snuggly-type carriers," Amy suggested. She grinned. "I wish I could design one. I'd make sure it was really radical. You know, extra pockets for all the important stuff—like guitar picks."

"Can you imagine," Palmer said, laughing, "Maggie and

63

Dan with a little punk baby? His hair would be spiked, and he'd have this tough little black leather jacket."

"And extremely cool shades that he'd always wear indoors," Amy added.

"And a tiny electric guitar," Palmer said. "With a lightning bolt on it."

"That's it!" Max said, smiling for the first time since Gracie had disappeared.

"A little electric guitar?" Shanon asked.

"No, silly. A giant teddy bear."

"Where did that come from?" Amy wondered.

"Who cares?" said Shanon. "I think it's the perfect gift." And so did everyone else.

Much later that night as Amy got ready to go to sleep she realized that for a while there, the four of them had been joking around, having a good time the way they used to. For a few minutes it had actually felt as if the Foxes of the Third Dimension were back.

Math was Palmer's last class of the day. She gathered up her books as the bell rang, still feeling a warm glow from the night before. It wasn't as if she and Amy had suddenly become best friends or anything, but she no longer felt as if everyone in 3-D hated her. She felt like one of the Foxes again. She hadn't realized how much she'd missed that.

For the first time in almost a month Palmer was looking forward to going back to the suite. They were all supposed to meet there at three o'clock, so they could get the posters photocopied and begin putting them up. *I'll just stop by Booth Hall first*, Palmer thought. If they all got mail from their pen pals, everything really would be perfect.

A few minutes later Palmer flipped through a handful of

envelopes. Amy had gotten a letter from her friend Evon, who lived in Australia. There was one for Shanon from Mars. Max had one from her youngest brother—no one else could possibly have handwriting that bad.

And there were three for Palmer. She gave a little squeal of delight as she saw that the first was from Max's cousin Rain Blackburn. *Well, he ought to write*, she told herself, trying not to get too carried away. *I've only sent him about a million letters*. The second letter was from Sam, and Palmer felt a flicker of guilt. Shanon had told her that he'd asked about her yesterday, and that he was worried about her. *I'll just have to write and tell him there's no future for us*, Palmer resolved. But she knew it wouldn't be an easy letter to write.

Palmer looked at the return address on the third letter, and thought her heart was going to stop beating. It was from Paul Grant. Gorgeous, wealthy Paul Grant had answered her letter!

This is too great, Palmer thought. *I can't stand it. I've got to tell someone*. But who? Obviously, this was one letter that she couldn't share with the Foxes. Come to think of it, she wasn't about to read Sam's letter aloud, either. Then again, she just might frame Rain Blackburn's and hang it in the sitting room. But it was Paul Grant's letter that seemed to tease her, daring her to open it.

Palmer took a deep breath. She knew what she was going to do. It meant she would be a little late for the three o'clock meeting, but her suitemates would just have to understand. Without another thought, she headed for Germaine's room.

CHAPTER EIGHT

———⟨●⟩———

Dear Palmer,

It was really nice of you to write, and yes, I could definitely use some advice on how to reach Max Schloss. She hasn't written back to me, so I guess my first letter didn't go over too well. The truth is, I didn't even write it. Believe it or not, I'd never written to a girl before, and I wasn't sure what to say. So I got this guy in my dorm to do it for me. He laid it on a little thick, huh?

If you could let me know what Max likes or is interested in, maybe I'll get my courage up and actually write her a letter myself. Thanks again for all your help.

Sincerely,
Paul Grant

Germaine gave a low, admiring whistle. "I've got to hand it to you, Palmer. You set this one up like a master. It may even be art."

"Art?" Reid echoed.

"It's brilliant," Germaine explained. "Now Palmer's got the perfect excuse for writing to Paul Grant. Plus he thinks she's some sort of guardian angel."

Palmer felt herself blushing at the unexpected praise—and wondering for a moment if she'd really been as manipulative as Germaine said. *Max doesn't like Paul Grant,* she reminded herself. *His crush on her is totally hopeless.* Technically, Palmer was stealing him, but in reality, she knew that she was saving everyone a lot of heartbreak. Now that she thought about it, Paul *and* Max ought to thank her for this!

"I just have one question," Germaine went on. "Once you get Paul Grant—and you will, of course—how are you going to get used to his face?"

That does it! Palmer thought furiously. *I have had it with Germaine making fun of Paul Grant's looks.* "I'll tell you what," she said, matching Germaine's cool tone. "I'm going to write to Paul, saying that Max wants a picture of him but is too shy to ask. Then you can see for yourself what he looks like."

Germaine went to the efficiency refrigerator in the corner of her room and took out a bottle of imported spring water. "Fine," she said. She opened a small cherry-wood cabinet, removed three crystal glasses, filled them with water, and gave one each to Palmer and Reid. "A toast," she announced, "to the new and improved Paul Grant."

"Cheers!" Palmer said.

Germaine's eyes slid to Reid. "Another toast to John Adams?"

Reid set her glass down on the top of the refrigerator and slouched against the wall. "I don't know," she said sullenly. "I wrote him, telling him I'd seen his poetry in the literary magazine, but he hasn't written back yet."

Palmer had to force herself not to laugh. John Adams always used to answer Amy's letters the day they arrived.

"Well then, a toast to John Adams answering his mail," Germaine said.

Reid raised her glass.

"What about you?" Palmer asked Germaine.

Germaine shrugged. "I don't really think this pen pals stuff is for me," she said. "But that's all right. I've got a date next week with my brother's college roommate. I told Maggie I was having dinner with my parents, and she gave me a pass. By the way, Palmer, have you heard from your parents about this summer?"

"My parents said I could go," Reid said.

Now that's something I'd better think about, Palmer realized. *Four weeks on a boat with Reid!* "Uh . . . my dad's away on business and my mother says she has to talk it over with him," she lied.

"Let me know," Germaine said. "In the meantime, hadn't you better go write Paulie Pig? I mean, how long are you going to keep matchmaking for Max?"

Palmer nearly spit out her imported water. "Matchmaking? What are you talking about?"

"Well," said Germaine, "Paul thinks you're about to tell him how to win Max Schloss. What *are* you going to tell him?"

"I'm not sure yet," Palmer admitted. For a moment she thought about the night before—how torn up Max had been about Gracie, and then the way they'd all helped out, kidding around again for the first time in weeks—how good it had felt.

"Just be honest," Reid said impatiently. "Tell him Max is weird—she's a loser."

"That's not subtle enough," Germaine disagreed. "He won't think Palmer's nice anymore."

"I'm not telling him Max is a loser," Palmer said. "Max has enough problems right now. The thing is, she really doesn't like Paul. Do you know what she said about his first letter? 'Yuk!' So I really should help her out. I mean, this is the last thing she needs to deal with right now."

"Besides," Germaine added, "how much longer can *you* deal with dating a pizza delivery boy?"

At the mention of Sam, Palmer felt the same sick feeling she'd gotten when she'd read his letter aloud.

"Remember," Germaine said softly. "All's fair in love and war. Here." She handed Palmer a sheet of white stationery. "Write to Paul now. All you have to do is steer him in the right direction. And believe me, if you can get past his looks, Paul Grant is worth it."

Palmer shot Germaine an annoyed glance but took the piece of paper. She thought for a moment, and then started writing.

Dear Paul:

I think Max is very lucky that someone like you wants to be her pen pal. You're right. Your first letter was a little much. But don't worry, I'm going to give you the key to Max Schloss's heart in three little words:

Max Schloss, Sr.

You see, Max has always been real close to her father. If you want Max to like you, then you'd better be a real fan of her dad and his show. It's practically her favorite subject in the entire world.

Don't get discouraged. Max is just shy. I think she likes you because yesterday she let it slip that she wished she had a picture of you. Of course, she'd never ask you directly. So if you just send it to me, I'll see that she gets it.

Let me know what happens. I'm always willing to help.

> *Sincerely,*
> *Your friend Palmer*

She handed the letter to Germaine. "Well?"

Germaine read quickly, then gave a low laugh. "I've got to hand it to you," she said. "At this rate you won't be on my yacht this summer—you'll be sailing the high seas with Paul!"

"Going to turn it all around now," Amy sang softly to herself. She changed keys and started singing again, this time drawing a fuller sound from the guitar.

> "Going to steal away somewhere
> they'll never find me
> Inside the place of dreams"

She shook her head. That didn't sound right. Too abstract and too clichéd. Still, there was something in the music that was real—something that spoke the truth about wanting to be in a place where the ordinary boundaries dissolved.

What a thing to write now, she thought ruefully. This was one of the rare times when she was glad to be exactly where she was. A soft spring rain fell outside. It felt so good to be alone in the suite, sitting on her bed, just listening to the rain and playing her guitar. Between softball practice and trying to avoid Palmer, it seemed as if it had been ages since she'd had time for herself.

She decided to try something different, and played an

old Beatles song about the rain. By the last verse she was singing at the top of her lungs. She collapsed on the bed, giggling, and then lay staring at the ceiling until she got her breath back.

When was the last time I sang full out like that? she wondered. *Not since I auditioned for Emmett's band.* She'd been so excited about singing with the Heartbreak. It would be so great if she could go to one of their concerts. She closed her eyes, imagining Emmett seeing her in the audience and pulling her onstage. "I want to introduce someone very special," he would say. "This is Amy Ho, the girl who was born to sing lead for this band. Amy, will you do a few numbers with us?" And then she and Emmett would bring down the house.

Amy sat up abruptly, her peaceful mood wrecked by her own fantasies. Thinking about Emmett made her excited and sad all at once. And she was still angry with Palmer, even though they'd been getting along for the last twenty-four hours. *Forget Palmer,* she told herself sternly. *That's in the past. What do you want to do now?*

I still want to make music with Emmett, she thought to herself. The very idea sent her heart racing. She wondered if Emmett even remembered her. Well, maybe it was time to remind him. She set the guitar gently in its case and rummaged through one of her desk drawers until she found a purple pad and a silver marker. She loved writing in silver. She thought awhile and then wrote:

Dear Emmett,
Long time no hear . . . but I haven't forgotten. I saw a poster for the band in Brighton, and all the music came back. I can almost hear how good the Heartbreak must

71

sound by now. Are you still playing those long, wild solos? Have you written a lot of new songs?

Although life at Alma Stephens isn't nearly as exciting as being in a band, a lot has happened lately. I'm playing catcher for our softball team. The team is incredible—so far, we're undefeated. Also, I'm still taking voice lessons with Professor Bernard. Mostly, he has me sing scales and voice exercises. So I've got to do all my rocking out on my own time. That's okay, though. I've written about three new songs since the last time I saw you.

Emmett, I really hope I can hear you play sometime soon. I know you're busy with the band and all, but if you want to get in touch, you can write me care of Fox Hall at Alma.

> *Rock on,*
> *Amy*

Amy read the letter over, wondering if it sounded too young or too dumb. She couldn't tell. She sealed the letter in an envelope and addressed it to Emmett. Then she took her guitar back out of its case and began to play.

Palmer found an empty table at the back of the Tuck Shop, set down her chocolate milkshake, and took two letters from her purse. Yesterday, after stopping in Germaine's room, she'd just caught the other Foxes as they were leaving 3-D to put up the posters. There'd been no time to read the mail, and by the time they got back dinner was being served. She'd actually forgotten about the two other letters she'd received yesterday until now. She couldn't wait any longer to see what Rain Blackburn had to say. And she had a funny feeling about Sam's letter. She didn't want anyone around when she read it. She opened Rain's first.

Dear Palmer:

Thanks for all your letters. I don't know how you do it. If I wrote that many letters, I'd never get any schoolwork done.

To answer some of your questions: Yes, I'm still playing music. No, I don't have a Mercedes. (And neither does my father.) No, I don't think I'll be in New Hampshire anytime soon. My favorite color is iridescent green. And yes, I do have a girlfriend. Her name is Mona. You'd probably like each other.

Got to go now. Say hi to Max and Amy and Shanon for me.

Be good,
Rain

"Hmmph!" Palmer said under her breath. She didn't know what made her angriest: Rain's having a girlfriend named Mona, his thinking they'd like each other, or his telling her to be good, as if she were a child! *I don't think I'll frame this letter, after all*, she decided.

She helped herself to a spoonful of milkshake and decided she couldn't put off the inevitable any longer. She opened Sam's letter.

Dear Palmer,

I guess you know all about Gracie disappearing the other day. It was pretty awful. Max looked like she wanted to die. If it's any help, everyone who's delivering pizza for Figaro's has been looking for her. I keep thinking some-

one's got to find her soon. *Tell Max not to give up.*

So now we come to the real reason for this letter. What's happening with you and me? Why haven't you answered my letters? If there's a problem, at least be straight with me. I thought the one thing you and I had was that we're honest with each other.

Look, I'm sorry. I don't want to yell at you in a letter (especially since I don't even know if I have a reason— what is going on????), so I'll sign off now.

> *Write to me, Palmer. I don't want to lose you.*
> *Sam*

P.S. *You still haven't heard the new song I wrote for you. We'll be playing it in the park next Sunday. Any chance you'll be there?*

Not a chance, Palmer thought, but her hands were trembling. Why couldn't Sam just get the message? She hadn't answered his letters. Obviously, she didn't want to be pen pals anymore. It wasn't very complicated. Why couldn't he figure it out?

For a moment she considered doing what he asked: leveling with him. But writing to pen pals was supposed to be fun. She wasn't about to turn it into torture.

She put the two letters back in her bag. *This is too grim,* she thought. *Paul Grant, you've just got to come through for me!*

CHAPTER NINE

Shanon swept into 3-D, her arms filled with books. She had another article to write for *The Ledger*, a French essay to translate, and somehow she'd let Dan Griffith talk her into doing an extra-credit paper for English. She hadn't even stopped by Booth Hall to check the mail; she wanted to get in at least two hours of studying before dinner. She dropped the books onto the desk in the sitting room and began searching for a pen that wasn't out of ink. Shanon was jinxed when it came to pens. Every time she picked one up, it conveniently decided it would never write again.

"Do you really need all those books?" asked Palmer.

Shanon turned around, wondering how she could have missed her suitemate. Palmer's hair was curled around dozens of skinny pastel hot rollers. She had a mint-green masque drying on her face, and tissues stuck between her toes—so the bright red polish wouldn't smudge. "Well," Palmer said, "I worry about you walking around campus, looking like a total nerd."

"That's nice of you," Shanon said. "Honestly, Palmer,

you make it sound like *I'm* the one who's weird. Do you have any idea of what you look like right now?"

"Consider this my homework," Palmer explained with an airy wave. "You know, looking the way I do isn't easy. It takes research, preparation, planning, attention to detail—"

"Money," Shanon supplied, grinning.

"Definitely. Two ounces of this masque cost almost fifty dollars."

"What?" Shanon yelped.

"Trust me," Palmer said, "it's worth it."

The door to the suite opened and Max walked in. "Good grief," she said, glancing at Palmer, "I never believed in aliens before this!"

"Ha ha," Palmer said.

"Have either of you heard anything about Gracie?" Max asked eagerly.

"Sorry," said Shanon. "No news today."

"Oh." Max sat down on the pink loveseat, her red tartan plaid skirt clashing wildly with the upholstery. "I can't even bear going to English anymore. Every time I look at Dan Griffith, I feel like the world's biggest creep. He must be standing up there, thinking, *There's Max Schloss, the girl who lost our dog.*"

"That's crazy," Shanon said. "You know he doesn't blame you. He even said so."

"He ought to," Max said in a whisper. "I do."

Palmer rolled her eyes and handed Shanon and Max an envelope apiece. "You're both a lot of fun today," she said irritably. "Don't you even want to know what your pen pals have to say?"

"Mars wrote!" Shanon said, smiling.

76

Palmer adjusted her white monogrammed robe and sat down in an armchair. "Go ahead, you start."

"What about Amy?" Max asked.

"Softball practice," Shanon said. "For a change."

Max shrugged. "We might as well wait."

"I thought you cared about Gracie," Palmer said indignantly. "Last week I put that ad about Gracie in the Ardsley *Lion*. Maybe one of these letters has news."

"I didn't think of that," Max said, her eyes brightening.

"That's why you need me," Palmer said. "I'm the one who makes things happen around here."

"Listen to this," Shanon demanded.

Dear Shanon,

Sound the trumpets—the infirmary has pronounced me totally cured at last! Not even a sniffle. Actually, I think they just got sick of seeing me. The feeling was entirely mutual. This means I'll definitely be at the play-off game between Alma Stephens and Brier Hall. I hear Amy is burning up the diamond.

You'll be glad to know all of The Unknowns are hot on the trail of Gracie Grayson-Griffith. We copied one of your posters and put it up all over Ardsley. Personally, I'm perfecting my secret whistle that only dogs can hear. I mean, it's not easy whistling at a decibel level I can't hear, but I'm sure it can be done.

Any word on our other case—The Mystery of the Reluctant Schloss? Paul keeps asking me if I think she hates his guts. She doesn't, does she?

"Stop right there!" Max ordered. "What did you tell him? You promised me you wouldn't say any—"

"Mars asked me about you and Paul before we had our talk," Shanon explained. "I told him I thought you liked Paul, but that's all. I haven't said a word to him since. Honest."

"I thought you couldn't stand Paul," Palmer said innocently.

"Oh, forget it," Max sighed.

"No can do." Palmer muttered under her breath. She checked her watch and began to unwind the curlers from her hair. Long golden waves fell to just beneath her shoulders. "You have to read your letter—it's from Paul," she added cheerfully.

Max looked at the ceiling, as if hoping for help from the heavens. When none arrived, she gave a deep sigh and opened the envelope.

Dear Max,

Since you haven't written back to me, I'm guessing my first letter laid it on a little too thick. I'm sorry. I haven't had much practice at being a pen pal. Could we start over? Maybe talk about something we're both interested in? Like the weather (just kidding) or maybe your dad's show. I've been a fan since I was about six. He is definitely the funniest man on TV. I've memorized entire routines of his. My sister says I do a great Christina Jean Queen. I'll do it for you sometime.

So what's it like being the daughter of Max Schloss? Is he as funny at home? Does he try out the new routines on the family? You know, you're the first girl whose father I've ever wanted to meet. Maybe we could all get together sometime. He and I could do Christina Jean Queen together.

Max stopped reading, jumped up, and screamed. "I knew it! I knew it! He's exactly like three fourths of the people I meet. The only reason he's interested in me is because he thinks I'll provide an instant introduction to my father. Or better yet, get him an audition. He doesn't want to know anything about *me*. All his questions are about my father. And Christina Jean Queen! Christina Jean Queen! That has got to be the most humiliating character my father's ever created! Oh, that would be a wonderful evening out—watching the *two* of them do Christina Jean Queen. I'd rather never have a date in my entire life!"

"You dropped this," Palmer said, stooping to pick up the photograph that had fallen out of Paul's letter.

"Keep it," Max snapped. "I never want to see his face again." She stormed into her room and returned a moment later with a pad and a pen. "Dear Groupie Grant," she said as she wrote. "You've been writing to the wrong person. Since you're obviously more interested in my father than you are in me, I'll give you what you really want—the address of his fan club. You might even get a signed photograph of him, if you're lucky. Sincerely, the daughter of someone famous."

"Max—" Shanon began.

"I don't want to hear it," Max said, brushing back tears. "I'm going for a walk."

"Whew!" Palmer said as the door to the suite slammed closed. "I guess she hates his guts after all."

"It doesn't make sense," Shanon mused. "Mars says Paul is a great guy. Not the kind who would use Max just to meet her father."

Palmer removed the tissues from between her toes. "Celebrity makes people do strange things," she said.

"I guess." Shanon looked at her watch. "Great. Dinner's only an hour away, and I still haven't opened a book." She shook her head, but couldn't help smiling at her suitemate. "You are a major distraction."

Palmer smiled back, clearly taking it as a compliment. "I know."

Shanon lifted her French book from the pile on the desk. "I think I'll go to the language lab. It's safer there."

"*Ciao,*" Palmer said. Alone in the suite, she washed the green masque off her face, checked that her skin really did look like satin (as the masque had promised it would), then brushed out her hair. Then she chose a piece of lavender stationery and began a letter of her own:

Dear Paul:

I heard about Max's reaction to your letter, and I wanted to tell you I'm really sorry. Please don't hold it against her. Ever since Gracie disappeared, Max has been very moody. It was kind of her fault, and she can't forgive herself.

I've been thinking—the Foxes and The Unknowns have always been friends, so if you still want a pen pal, I'd be glad to write to you (even though I already have two pen pals).

Your friend,
Palmer
P.S. Max wasn't too excited about your photograph, but I think it's great.

That evening Palmer stood on line in the dining hall, barely noticing the dish of goulash that Mrs. Butter set on her tray. She peered around a tall girl who stood in front of her, trying to see if she could spot Germaine. Amy and

80

Max and Shanon were sitting at a table near the window with Muffin Talbot and Kate Majors. Reid Olivier was sitting by herself near the back wall. That meant that Germaine hadn't shown up yet. Palmer took a piece of angel food cake for dessert, and wondered if she could stomach sitting with Reid until Germaine showed up. It was definitely worth it. She *had* to show Germaine the picture of Paul Grant.

"Hi," she said, taking a place across the table from Reid.

Reid looked up from some sort of list lying next to her plate. "Hi," she said. She nodded at the list. "I'm trying to figure out what clothes I need to buy for this summer. Did your parents give you permission yet?"

"Not yet," Palmer answered. The truth was she was torn. One part of her imagined a glamorous trip, sailing with the Richardses, docking at exotic ports, dancing under a tropical moon, buying souvenirs that would make Georgette green with envy. The other part of her couldn't imagine lasting a day on the yacht without pushing Reid Olivier overboard. Germaine got on her nerves now and then, but Reid was like a fingernail scraping across a blackboard.

"I was thinking," Reid continued, "that I should get something silk and strapless for evening."

"Probably," Palmer said, barely listening. She hadn't even asked her parents yet. That would be another problem. Even if she had to share her dad with Georgette, she wasn't sure she wanted to give up her time with him this summer.

"I already have black sandals with ankle straps and heels," Reid went on, "but I bet I'll need white as well." She pointed a finger at Palmer. "You have those gorgeous white sandals from Milan. If you come, maybe I'll borrow those."

Palmer nearly choked on a brussels sprout.

"So," Germaine said, setting down her tray, "junior jock Lenny Callen just sent me another one of his fascinating letters. Thank goodness he skipped the poetry this time. Now, I know how you get pen pals, but how do you get rid of them?"

Palmer winced at the question. It reminded her of Sam. "I don't know," she said, staring at her goulash. "Don't answer his letters, I guess. He'll get the message."

"Will he?" Germaine asked pointedly, and for a second Palmer could have sworn that Germaine was really asking about Sam.

"Tell him you've already picked another, better pen pal," Reid suggested.

That, too, hit a little close to home, and Palmer spoke up quickly, "I thought you'd want to see what I got in the mail today." She handed Germaine Paul Grant's photograph.

Germaine was silent for a moment and then gave a low, throaty laugh. "My, my . . . the baby pig grew up, and he's not half-bad. Not *my* taste, but not bad." She regarded Palmer with something that might have been respect. "So your plan worked. He's your pen pal now?"

Palmer shrugged and tried not to look too pleased with herself. "Max didn't like him," she said. "They really didn't have anything in common."

Max walked along the river's edge, watching as a family of ducks swam by in a smooth, effortless line, each duck seeming to know exactly where it was meant to be. "How

82

come you know exactly what to do, and my life is such a mess?" she asked them.

What Max really couldn't understand was how she could have been so wrong about Paul. Maybe she'd imagined the Valentine's Day Dance. The Paul Grant she remembered dancing with wouldn't have written that first mushy letter, and he certainly wouldn't have tried to use her.

Why am I wasting all this time thinking about Paul Grant anyway? Max asked herself. *I already have a perfectly great pen pal. Writing to Jose should be more than enough.*

But it wasn't, and Max knew it.

CHAPTER TEN

Palmer took a deep breath, trying not to let the disappointment show. Removing the sweatbands from her wrists, she began to walk off the tennis court. Alma had just lost its seventh straight match. *Thank you, Jeannie Lawson.* Palmer stopped at the edge of the court in surprise. There was loud applause coming from the sidelines, and it was for her! She smiled and waved at the crowd. She'd played her heart out and everyone knew it. It wasn't the same as winning, but it made her feel good.

Georgette detached herself from the crowd and appeared at Palmer's side. "You were fantastic! For a while there it looked as if you were going to win the match single-handedly."

Palmer's good mood faded. "Well, I didn't," she said. "We were playing doubles. That means two people have to play well."

"I think Jeannie Lawson should be kicked off the team," Georgette said loyally.

"So do I," Palmer agreed, "but who would replace her? No one else is much better . . . though at least the others show up for practice."

"Uh . . . Palmer," Georgette said.

Palmer's eyes narrowed as she looked down at her stepsister. "What?"

"I got a letter from Sam the other day."

Palmer didn't want to believe what she'd just heard. "Sam O'Leary?"

Georgette nodded.

"Why on earth would he write to you?"

"Because he's worried about you!" Georgette said indignantly. "He wrote to me because he thought I might know if he'd done anything to make you mad."

"Oh, that's just great," Palmer said. She slung her tennis bag over her shoulder and headed for the showers.

"Well," Georgette persisted, "did he?"

"I already told you, it's none of your business."

"It became my business when Sam wrote to me," Georgette pointed out. "What did he do?"

"Nothing," Palmer snapped, jerking open the door to the gym. "I'm just not interested in writing to him anymore."

Georgette trailed behind her into the locker room. "Okay, maybe what you said last time is right—things are changing."

"I've got to take a shower now," Palmer muttered.

"So," Georgette concluded cheerfully, "if you don't want to be Sam's pen pal anymore, I do."

Palmer stared at her stepsister in disbelief. *First she gets my father. Now she wants Sam.* "Georgette," Palmer said, slowly and distinctly, "I can take care of my own pen pals. If you want a pen pal, find your own. Stop trying to take over everything that's mine!"

"Pen pals," Georgette repeated thoughtfully. "You mean

85

Sam and Rain?"

Palmer couldn't resist bragging. "Plus someone even cuter and more interesting."

Georgette's blue eyes, so much like Palmer's, widened with understanding. "So that's why you don't want to write to him anymore," she said softly. "Oh, Palmer, how could you do that to Sam?"

Palmer put her racket in her locker, slammed the metal door closed, and spun the combination lock furiously. "What are you, my conscience?"

Georgette drew herself up with dignity. "You don't have to worry. I won't say a word about this to Sam. You're going to have to get yourself out of this one!"

Palmer hesitated before opening the door to suite 3-D. She didn't really want to report another tennis disaster to her suitemates. Then again, she probably wouldn't have to; anyone who knew anything about Alma's tennis team expected disaster. She tried to remember if Amy had had a game as well. No, thank goodness. This week the softball team played on Saturday.

She found Max in the sitting room, legs propped high against the wall, back on the floor, and holding an open book about six inches above her face. "What are you doing?" Palmer asked.

"Studying. Or, if you'd like me to be specific, discovering that I never really wanted to know what a gerund was anyway. Can any subject in the universe be more boring than grammar?"

"Latin," Palmer said.

Max turned her head to look at Palmer. "It didn't go so well, did it?"

"You must be psychic," Palmer muttered.

Max looked at her sympathetically. "You know, you really ought to let us come to a match. It might help if we were cheering you on."

"Oh, please," Palmer said. "I'd rather not have everyone watch me make a fool of myself once a week."

Max grinned. "Don't be so self-conscious. We all get to watch each other make fools of ourselves. At least once a week."

The door to the suite opened, and Amy came in, wearing black high tops, a short, black denim skirt, a white T-shirt, and a black vest.

"Mail call," Amy announced, taking a few envelopes from her pack. "Let's see what we have here . . . a letter from your parents," she said to Max. "And one from mine." She gave Palmer a wry grin. "I can remember when the mail around here used to be more exciting." She looked at the third envelope and frowned. "Palmer, why is Paul Grant writing to you?"

Palmer felt a surge of panic, which was immediately replaced by one of indignation. Who was Amy Ho to question her about anything? "Why shouldn't Paul Grant write to me?" she replied. "It's a free country, isn't it?"

Amy looked questioningly at Max. "I thought you liked Paul. What happened?"

Max lowered the open grammar book over her face.

Amy removed the book. "Talk to me. What's going on?"

With a sigh of defeat, Maxie sat up. "Paul Grant sent me another letter," she reported without emotion. "It was a nightmare. All he talked about was how much he admires my father. How he does Christina Jean Queen imitations, and how what he'd really like to do most in life is get together with my dad and do comedy routines with him. It couldn't have been worse. It was like someone gave him a secret formula for what I hate most."

Amy was silent for a moment, then she looked up at Palmer. "Maybe someone did."

Max's head snapped up. "What's that supposed to mean?"

But Amy didn't answer. All her attention was focused on her roommate. "All right, Palmer, don't you think it's time you shared Paul's letter with the rest of 3-D?"

"Sha—Shanon isn't here," Palmer stammered.

"That's okay," Amy said. "We'll make an exception this time."

"No!" Palmer said, stamping her foot. "You can't force me to do anything."

"Sooner or later you know you'll have to read it," Amy told her.

"And if I don't?"

Amy shrugged. "If you don't, I'll write to Paul Grant. I'll tell him about some of the stuff you've pulled in the past, and then I'll ask him what's been going on. If I were you, I'd save myself the embarrassment."

"That's blackmail!" Palmer said furiously.

"Call it what you like."

"Amy," said Max, standing up, "what are you—"

"Read it, Palmer," Amy cut her off. "Read it now or I write to Paul Grant."

Palmer felt herself turning red as she realized there was no way out of this one. "All right," she said in the coolest tone she could manage. "I'll read it—and then you'll realize how horrible you've been to me, Amy Ho!"

Amy did not look impressed. "Just read it and save the theatrics."

Palmer swallowed hard, opened Paul Grant's letter, and took a deep breath.

Dear Palmer:

Thanks for offering to be my pen pal. I guess I'd like to take you up on it, since it's obviously not happening with Max Schloss. I never wanted to give up on her, but how can I be pen pals with someone who likes guys who are into her father's show and then acts like a complete snob and tells me to write his fan club?

"Likes guys who are into my father's show?" Max echoed in a strangled voice. "Where would he ever get an idea like that?"

"I'll give you one guess," Amy snapped.

"It was obvious that Max didn't like him," Palmer said. "I was just trying to spare everyone a lot of grief."

"No," Amy said. "You were just trying to take him for yourself. You have absolutely no morals."

"I do, too!" Palmer insisted.

"Really? Then why don't you explain how you can steal a friend's pen pal— not once but twice!"

"Twice?" Max echoed.

"She's done it before," Amy said, her voice filled with contempt. "She's always butting into everyone's life and rearranging things for her own convenience. She is the most selfish person on the planet!"

"And you hold a grudge longer than anyone in the universe!" Palmer retorted.

"At least I know how to be a friend," Amy said, her

voice suddenly quiet. "That's the part I really can't understand. All of us in 3-D have been through so much together. But that doesn't seem to mean anything to you. We thought you were our friend. The truth is, you can't be trusted. You can't be trusted at all."

"Just a minute," Palmer sputtered. "Max didn't want to be Paul's pen pal. She hated his first letter. She doesn't like him—she doesn't even like boys! She said so." Palmer turned to Max. "Didn't you?"

"I—I—" Max wondered if it was possible to die of embarrassment. Amy and Palmer were staring at her, waiting for an answer. Somehow she couldn't bring herself to admit that she had a crush on Paul Grant. "It's really no big deal," she insisted, wishing both her suitemates would disappear and leave her to her own misery. "I—"

A knock on the door cut her off.

"Oh, no," Max groaned. "I totally forgot about the pizza. Do you think they'll take it back? I can't eat after this—I think my appetite's been permanently destroyed."

Amy opened the door. Sam O'Leary stood there, a pizza box in his hand. His eyes went to Palmer's, searching, as if by looking hard enough he could somehow read her heart.

Palmer turned a pale shade of green.

For a long moment no one spoke, then Sam thrust the pizza box at Palmer and said, "Just give me my $9.75, and we won't have to see each other again."

"I—I'm the one who ordered it," Max stammered, handing him the money.

Sam's eyes were still fixed on Palmer, and for the first time since she'd known him, there was no warmth in them. He was looking at her as if she were a stranger. Without another word he turned and left.

Palmer stood absolutely paralyzed. Then she dropped the box and dashed out after Sam.

She had never run after a boy in her life, but she couldn't let Sam go—not like that. She raced down the stairs and out of Fox Hall. Ahead of her, Sam was crossing the quad with swift, angry strides. "Sam, wait!" she shouted. "We have to talk! Please!"

Sam stopped, but he kept his back to her.

"Listen," she said, grabbing his arm and turning him to face her. "I'm sorry I didn't answer your letters. It's just that I—" What could she say? "I was real busy with classes and all. We got a lot of homework and I had to do a makeup paper and Shanon was tutoring me in Latin and—"

"Palmer, don't. Don't make it worse by telling me a bunch of lies." To her surprise Sam didn't sound angry; he just sounded tired.

"But I want to explain," she protested.

"You don't have to explain. It's not that mysterious. You think I didn't realize that you stopped writing after I said I couldn't take you to the concert? I mean, I was trying to give you every chance under the sun—I *wanted* it to be something like too much homework—but did you really think I wouldn't figure it out? And you didn't even have the guts to be straight with me."

"Sam, please—"

He shook her arm off with a sharp, hard movement. "No. It's exactly like when we first met. We still have that one major problem: I'm not rich enough for you. But you know what? That's okay. I figure we're even—you're not nice enough for me."

This time when he left she didn't try to stop him.

91

CHAPTER ELEVEN

———◆———

Palmer sank down onto the grass, stunned. Around her Alma students were walking along the quad, talking and laughing, complaining about their classes and gossiping with their friends. But all Palmer could see was an image of Sam, standing there in front of her, allowing her to see all the hurt she'd caused him. Yes, she'd lost interest in him as a pen pal, but she'd *never* wanted to hurt him the way she had. She never thought it would come to this.

Shanon's friendly voice broke into her thoughts. "What are you doing, sitting here all by yourself? Don't tell me you've taken up meditation."

Palmer buried her head in her knees. The fight with Sam had been bad enough. But the one with Max and Amy was even worse. How could she ever go back to 3-D?

"Palmer?" She felt Shanon's hand on her shoulder. "What's wrong? Did something happen?"

Her kindness was more than Palmer could take. The tears started to fall.

"Palmer, what is it?"

"They hate me," Palmer sobbed.

"Who?"

"Everyone. Amy and Max and Sam . . . even Georgette."

Shanon knelt beside her. "Palmer, I can't stand to see you crying this way. Please tell me what happened."

Palmer picked her head up, sniffed loudly, and brushed away her tears. "It was just a misunderstanding," she mumbled.

"Do you really believe that, Palmer?"

"Okay, it was more than a misunderstanding," she admitted. "But I'm not ready to talk about it yet."

"Fair enough." Shanon stood up and held out her hand. "Come on. You can't stay out here. It's going to be dark soon."

Palmer shook her head. "I can't go back to 3-D."

Concern flickered in Shanon's eyes. "Was it really that bad?"

Palmer nodded miserably.

Shanon sighed and sat down beside her. "Then I guess I'll keep you company."

Palmer stared at her suitemate, amazed. "You would do that for me?"

"Sure."

A trace of a smile played at the corners of Palmer's mouth. "Then I guess I could get up the courage to go back in there."

Dear Mars,

Boy, are you glad you don't live in 3-D! We've progressed from a cool freeze to an all-out war zone. Without going into the messy details, let's just say that Amy and Max could cheerfully strangle Palmer, and Palmer's walking around like one of those soap-opera heroines who are always suffering a drawn-out, but highly dramatic (not to mention, photogenic), death. (She keeps striking these weird poses with the back of her hand against her forehead.) I guess I'm making it sound funny, but the truth is, things here have never been so depressing.

The reason I'm telling you all this is because part of the problem has to do with Max and Paul. Could you please tell Paul to disregard Max's last letter? She never meant to insult him, and she's writing him a letter now that will explain everything.

Are you still coming to the play-off game on Saturday? Alma lost for the first time yesterday, which means that we're even with Brier Hall again in the standings. (Amy says not to worry—we're gonna win the pennant.)

I'd better sign off now. Max is sitting across from me and Palmer just walked in. I may have to head them off at the pass.

> As they say at the U.N., "Peace,"
> Shanon

Dear Shanon,

Things at Alma sound as dreary as things here at home. Still, I wish I were there. I definitely want to come back next year. I miss Rob so much. He keeps writing me these great letters, asking when I'll be back. And I always want to say, "Tomorrow!" Have you seen him lately? Is he still as cute as ever?

I'm sorry things in 3-D are so awful, but even when I was there it seemed like Amy and Palmer were heading for a major clash. It may just be one of those unavoidables.

Life at home is—strange. My parents have definitely decided on a divorce. I always thought that would be the worst thing in the world, but now that it's actually happening I think I'm getting used to the idea. I still hate it and wish everything could be the way it was when I was little, but somehow becoming the child of "a broken home" is beginning to feel normal. I realize that Reggie and I are no different than millions of other kids. I just never thought I'd be one of them.

Next letter, I promise I will only write about cheerful topics. (At this rate, it'll be a very short letter.) Don't get too caught up in the Palmer/Amy war if you can possibly help it. And if you see Rob, tell him I miss him like crazy! I miss you, too.

Love,
Lisa

Dear Paul:

I hope you can forgive me for writing that awful letter and calling you Groupie Grant. You'll never believe what happened . . .

Dear Paul:

I think I owe you an explanation and an apology. The story starts with Palmer. No, I take that back. It really starts with me. When I got your first letter . . .

Dear Paul:

I wouldn't blame you if you hate my guts and never want to hear from me again, but I think you should know that we were set up . . .

Dear Paul:

How good is your sense of humor?

Max sat cross-legged on the loveseat, an open phone book on her lap.

"Who are you looking up?" asked Amy, emerging from her room with her catcher's mitt.

"Not who. What. I'm looking for stores in Brighton that sell toys. I figured that when I go to pick up Jose's turtle, I'd see if I could find the giant teddy bear for the baby."

"Still no word on Gracie?" Amy asked.

Max shook her head.

"You've got to stop feeling so guilty."

"I know," Max said in a small voice. "But I can't."

"Have you heard from Paul?"

"No, but that's because I haven't written to him yet. I mean, I've tried, but I can't figure out how to explain this whole mess and not have him think I'm even more of an idiot than I actually am."

"You're not an idiot," Amy said firmly. "You just had the bad luck to be sharing a suite with Palmer Durand."

"I heard that!" Palmer called out from her room.

"Stick around," Max called back. "You'll hear more."

Palmer charged out of her room, an open mascara wand in one hand. "I have put up with about all I can take from you two," she said angrily. Drops of mascara flew from the wand, and one of them landed squarely on Max's white sweater.

"Great, Palmer," said Max.

"I didn't mean—"

"No, let me guess," Amy interrupted. "You're going to tell us you did it for Max's own good. You're going to say you thought Max's sweater really *needed* a touch of mascara."

"That is totally unfair," Palmer said. "The mascara was an accident, and you know it!"

Max yawned. "Sure, Palmer. Anything you say."

"You don't believe me?" Palmer demanded, outraged.

"I already explained this," Amy said in a bored tone. "It's not that we don't believe you. It's that we don't trust you. You. Can't. Be. Trusted."

"That does it!" Palmer fumed. "That just does it! You've made it perfectly clear that I'm not welcome here, so I won't burden you with my presence any longer."

"Oh, please," said Max, "you sound like a bad soap opera."

Palmer swept into her room and returned moments later, carrying her makeup case, six of her favorite outfits, and her blow-drier. "If anyone wants to know," she huffed, "they can find me at Germaine's."

"Perfect," Amy observed. "You deserve each other."

Palmer yanked open the door to the suite, stepped over the threshold, and slammed the door shut. Two seconds later it opened again. "And there's another thing, Max Schloss," she shrieked. "I'm glad I got mascara on your sweater!"

For the fourth time Palmer knocked on Germaine's door. She wasn't even going to consider the possibility that Germaine was out and she'd be stuck standing in the hallway with all this stuff in her arms.

Germaine opened the door a crack and peered out. "Palmer, what in the world—"

"Will you just open the door?" Palmer snapped. "Why did you keep me waiting?"

97

"I was taking a nap," Germaine said, letting her in. "I didn't want to be disturbed."

Palmer bit back an angry retort. After all, she needed Germaine's help. "Sorry," she said, "but I didn't have a choice. Germaine, can I stay here?"

Germaine adjusted the tie on her silk robe. "For how long?"

"I don't know," Palmer said honestly. "All I know is I can't spend another minute with Amy Ho and Max Schloss."

"Well, that's perfectly understandable."

"They are so mean. Do you know what Amy said to me?" Palmer demanded, still stung by the argument. "She said I can't be trusted. After all I've done for her!"

Germaine waved to a corner of the room. "You can put your stuff there, on the floor next to my dresser, but make sure it's neat."

"I—I thought I'd hang my clothes up in the closet," Palmer said.

"There's no room," Germaine said quickly. She opened the large wooden chest at the foot of her bed and took out extra sheets, blankets, and a pillow. "And you can sleep over there." She pointed to a space on the floor next to the refrigerator. "Don't worry. The rug is nice and thick."

"Germaine—" Palmer began.

"Look," Germaine said, "I'm sorry this isn't as spacious as a suite, but you know the private rooms here are small. We'll just have to do the best we can. Did you bring a nightgown? No? I can lend you a T-shirt."

"Thanks," Palmer said. "Thanks a lot."

Palmer turned over restlessly, sure that the sculptured

pattern of Germaine's carpet was leaving a permanent impression on her skin. Germaine had fallen asleep hours ago. But every time Palmer started to drift off, the refrigerator's motor turned itself on, waking her up again. She gave serious thought to unplugging the thing, and then decided she wasn't ready for a scene with Germaine in the morning. She'd had enough problems with roommates to last her a lifetime!

Palmer awoke the next morning looking at Paul Grant's picture. It took her a moment to remember that she'd set it on the floor beside her makeshift bed, so she'd have something comforting to look at in Germaine's room. Germaine was already dressed and standing in front of the mirror, brushing her hair.

"What time is it?" Palmer asked fuzzily.

"Eleven-thirty," Germaine answered. "I had an early lunch, so I decided to come back here and freshen up."

"You let me sleep till eleven-thirty?" Palmer wailed. "That means I missed my first three classes, and no one's going to give me a pass for it. I'll have detentions for the rest of the school year! How could you let me oversleep?"

Germaine shrugged. "I tried to wake you."

Palmer frantically struggled into her clothes and ran a brush through her hair. "I've got to go," she said to Germaine.

"I'll meet you later," Germaine said. "There's still something I need to do here."

When Palmer had gone Germaine walked over to where Palmer had slept and picked up the picture of Paul Grant. "Now that you don't look like a baby pig, I don't see why you should waste your time on Palmer," she mused aloud. She put the picture back and took out a sheet of plain white stationery. Her eyes were drawn back to Paul's picture. She thought for a moment, and then wrote in precise script:

Dear Paul:

I'm a friend of Palmer Durand's and I know that you two have been writing to each other. Palmer is, as I'm sure you've noticed, very charming, and she always means well. But I've lived in the same dorm with her for the last two years, and there's one thing everyone at Alma agrees on: Palmer Durand can't be trusted.

Believe me, this is a hard thing for me to write, because I like Palmer. But I thought you deserved fair warning. I'd hate to see anyone else get hurt by her lies.

Sincerely,
A friend

CHAPTER TWELVE

Max walked past the video games, badminton sets, and crafts projects toward the toy store's stuffed animal display. She blinked at the array of tigers, walruses, elephants, bears, rabbits, lions, dogs—there was even a little bat. She wondered briefly what sort of person would buy a stuffed bat for a child, and then focused on her mission: to find the perfect teddy bear for Maggie and Dan.

Originally, back when they all were still speaking to each other, the Foxes had planned to buy this gift together. But the way things were now, everyone had agreed that it would be the least hassle if Max picked out the bear herself when she was in town.

Max shook her head ruefully. This was supposed to be fun, but all it did was remind her of how awful everything was. The truth was she hated being mad at Palmer. She'd felt terrible a few days ago when she and Amy had ganged up on her. And it didn't help that Palmer was still staying with Germaine. Max had considered apologizing, but every time she did she remembered why she was angry with Palmer in the first place—and she couldn't seem to stop being angry. *There's got to be a way out of this*, she told herself. *We can't fight forever*. Even Shanon, who staunchly refused to take sides, seemed to be avoiding all of them. *I don't blame her*, Maxie thought. *I'd avoid us, too*.

In the meantime, there were half a dozen giant stuffed teddy bears to choose from. Max's eye immediately went to one wearing a jaunty red vest with a little plaid handkerchief sticking out of the vest pocket. He looked the friendliest, she decided. She carried him to the register, asked to have him delivered, and paid for him.

Then she set off for the pet store. This was even more depressing because she had to pass Figaro's on the way, and that brought back the awful memory of losing Gracie. Over the last few days Max had been trying to accept the fact that Gracie might never return. Despite the posters and phone calls and newspaper ads, there wasn't a single lead. No one had seen the little white terrier. *She couldn't have just vanished*, Max told herself. *Someone has her and they don't want to give her back*.

Inside the pet store, she paid for Jose's turtle, and at the last moment decided to buy a tank and a month's supply of turtle food as well. She would see Jose tomorrow, and give him his new pet. *See, there is a reason to go on living*, she told herself. Jose was one pen pal Max could count on for a long, long time.

Amy returned to 3-D floating on air. Alma had just met Brier Hall in the second of three play-off games. Brier Hall had taken the first, but Alma had taken—no *stolen*—this one. Amy tossed off her cap, collapsed into the easy chair, and closed her eyes. Instantly she was back on the softball field—in that sweet moment when she'd pegged a rope to second, thrown out a runner trying to steal a base, and won the game! They were going to win the final. She was sure of it!

She heard the sound of a key in the door and opened her eyes. Palmer walked in—probably for another one of her endless changes of clothing. Shanon had calculated that in the three days Palmer had stayed with Germaine she'd returned to 3-D for clothing at least four times a day. *She can do whatever she wants*, Amy thought. *Even Palmer Durand can't bring me down now.*

"Brilliant game," Palmer said coolly.

"Thanks," Amy replied, a little unsure of whether Palmer actually meant it. "Were you there?"

"I was there," Palmer said. "I was watching you, and realizing that I don't know you at all."

Amy sat up. "What's that supposed to mean?"

"It means that whatever our differences, I always thought you were someone who kept her word," Palmer said with a self-righteous sniff.

"I do," Amy said.

"No, you don't!" Palmer accused her. "You said you'd only blackmail me if I didn't read Paul Grant's letter to you and Max. So I read the letter to you, and you went ahead and blackmailed me anyway!"

"*What* are you talking about?" Amy asked, completely baffled.

"This," Palmer said, thrusting a letter at her. "Read it."

Amy took the letter and opened it.

Dear Palmer,
So I guess we're pen pals now. I asked Mars what pen

pals write about, and he says I should start by telling you stuff about me—like what kind of music I like. And I'll get to all that, but first there's something I think I should tell you. Only I'm not sure how.

Okay, here goes. Yesterday I got an anonymous letter from someone who claims to be your friend. She said that everyone at Alma knows you "can't be trusted." She warned me about not getting hurt by your lies!

I don't know who would have written a letter like that, but it was a rotten thing to do—especially since I know how nice you really are. I'm not telling you this to upset you. I'm telling you because I think you ought to be careful around the people who call themselves your friends.

Amy looked up from the letter, her face a mask of disbelief. "You think I sent Paul that letter?" she asked.

"Who else?" Palmer snapped. "You even told me you would."

Amy winced. "I only said that because I was mad. I never would have done it—even if you'd *hadn't* read Paul's letter to us."

Palmer's blue eyes flashed. "Why should I believe you? Here is the evidence!"

"Because," Amy said, "writing a letter like that would be exactly what Paul said it was—rotten. And I wouldn't stoop that low, no matter how angry I was."

"Really?" Palmer said. "If you ask me, both you and Max have stooped pretty low in the last week or so."

"Maybe," Amy agreed, silently adding, *and you deserved it.* "But that letter is something else. I didn't write it, and I can promise you Max didn't either.

"Then who did write it?" Palmer demanded.

104

"I don't know!" Amy said, getting tired of defending herself for something she hadn't done. "Why don't you think about some of your other 'friends,' and I don't mean Shanon."

"Because," Palmer said, "I have proof you wrote that letter. Those were your exact words: *You can't be trusted.* You said that to me twice. No one else would have written that."

Amy sighed, suddenly feeling all the exhaustion of the softball game hit her. "For the last time: I did not write that letter to Paul Grant. I have never written a letter to Paul Grant. And I have no idea who did write it."

"I don't believe you!" Palmer said.

Amy gave a helpless shrug. "Believe what you want."

Dear Max,

Thanks for the turtle! He is the greatest. We named him Speedy. Lila keeps asking him if he knows the Teenage Mutant Ninja Turtles. Even my foster parents think he's cute. They helped me find some good rocks to put in his tank. I like to talk to him every morning when I get up and every night before I go to sleep. He is very wise for a turtle. I'm going to ask him if he knows where Gracie is.

Your pen pal,
Jose (and Speedy, too!)

Dear Shanon:

I never thought that I, Mars Martinez, would be so grateful for softball games—but they're the perfect way to see you. (Plus we get to watch the Mighty Ho cream all those other teams.) I can't believe Alma's got only one more game left—that means we've either got to change the soft-

ball schedule or come up with some fresh excuses for seeing each other. Don't worry, I'm already working on it.

I thought you'd want to know that I talked to Paul about Max. You didn't give me a whole lot to go on, but I told him that something weird must have happened for Max to write a letter like that—it just isn't her style. I'm not sure I convinced him. He looked as confused as I am. And I don't think he ever got that letter where she explained everything. Did you know he's writing to Palmer now? And I saw Sam in town and he isn't. What is going on over there anyway? I know you're being a total diplomat and trying not to betray anyone's secrets, but we of The Unknown are going kind of crazy.

Still crazy about you,
Mars

P.S. See you at the final game!

Dear Paul:

I'm glad we're pen pals now. Your letter was great. We have exactly the same taste in music and videos and cars! And even though it was hard for me to find out that a friend had betrayed me, I was really glad you were so honest with me. The minute I saw your letter I knew exactly who that "friend" was. I showed her your letter. She was completely humiliated to have been caught at her own game. The important thing is that you didn't believe her.

Are you coming to the final softball game on Saturday? (After all these letters, isn't it time we got together again? I'm enclosing a picture to refresh your memory.)

See you in the bleachers,
Palmer

Palmer stood with her back to the softball field, her eyes scanning the stands. It was early, and people were still arriving, but she was sure Paul Grant was around somewhere. She was dressed casually—western boots, a short denim skirt, and a blue pin-striped shirt. She knew she looked good, even better than the picture she'd sent.

There he was! She spotted him walking through the main gate with Mars and Rob Williams. Shanon appeared, immediately reaching for Mars's hand, but talking to Rob. She was probably giving him the latest news from Lisa McGreevy. Palmer tossed her hair over her shoulder and began to saunter toward them.

Paul turned away from Mars and Rob and caught Palmer's eye as she walked up next to him. "Palmer," he said, sounding pleased to see her.

"Hi." Palmer gave him her brightest smile. "It's great to see you again," she gushed.

Paul looked slightly embarrassed. "You, too."

"Let's find seats," Palmer said eagerly. "We have so much to talk about."

But before they could do anything else, someone caught Paul by the arm. "Paul Grant, I can't believe it! I knew you were at Ardsley. How come we've never seen each other? You should have written to me."

"Germaine," Paul said. Palmer couldn't tell from Paul's tone of voice whether he was glad to see Germaine or not.

"Do you remember that summer on the Vineyard when you and I got stuck out in that skiff, and your mother called the Coast Guard?" Germaine went on, hooking an arm through Paul's. "There we were, all of twenty yards from shore and half the eastern fleet was searching for us.

107

By the way, how is your mother?" Palmer watched, astounded, as Germaine deftly led Paul away. And suddenly she knew exactly who'd written that letter.

"Looks like Germaine's rediscovered Paulie Pig," came a slightly nasal voice.

"Reid," Palmer said quickly, turning toward the older girl, "you're just the person I wanted to see."

Reid looked as surprised as someone who looked perpetually bored could look. One of her eyebrows lifted a fraction of an inch.

"Did Germaine write to Paul Grant?" Palmer asked.

"How would I know?"

"Because you know everything that Germaine does."

Reid smiled. "I do, don't I?"

"Did she write to him?" Palmer pressed.

Reid nervously brushed the shock of frizzy hair away from her left eye. "Let's just say . . . it's possible."

"How possible?"

Reid pretended to be fascinated by her nails. Then again, thought Palmer, maybe she really was. "Reid," she said patiently, "why did Germaine write to Paul? She doesn't like him, remember?"

Reluctantly, Reid looked up from her nails. "I guess she thought he'd changed enough."

Palmer gritted her teeth to keep from screaming. "Enough for what?"

"To go out with, of course. I mean, he's younger than she is, and all, but he's from a good family, and he isn't bad-looking now."

"I see," said Palmer. She wanted to knock both Germaine and Reid through the bleachers, but there was something she had to do first. She had to find Amy!

CHAPTER THIRTEEN

Palmer burst into the locker room and found Amy sitting on a bench. Her roommate was talking to Michelle, the outfielder, Amy's best friend on the softball team. "Thank goodness, you're still here," Palmer exclaimed. "I've *got* to talk to you!"

"Not now," Amy said without looking up. "Whatever it is, save it for after the game. I have to concentrate."

"It can't wait," Palmer said.

Amy mustered as much patience as she could manage. "Palmer, the final play-off game—the championship game—starts in exactly twenty minutes. I can't afford to be distracted now."

"This will help you!" Palmer insisted. "I promise."

Amy rolled her eyes. "You won't leave until you've said whatever it is you're dying to say, will you?"

Palmer grinned. "Not a chance."

Amy sighed loudly. "Okay, just do me a favor and get it over with."

Palmer took a deep breath. "I found out that Germaine

wrote that poison pen letter to Paul," she began. "I'd told her that you said I couldn't be trusted, and she used it in the letter. I'm sorry. I never should have accused you."

"Is that all you're sorry for?" Amy asked, completely unmoved by Palmer's apology.

Palmer knew what Amy was talking about. It hurt her pride to apologize for something that had felt okay at the time, but what mattered now was making things right with Amy. "I'm sorry about Emmett, too," she said quietly. "I shouldn't have interfered."

"Do you mean that?" Amy asked.

"Totally!" Palmer vowed. "I—I know I've messed things up for you. But honest, I only did it because I thought Emmett was going to hurt you."

"And?"

"And maybe because . . . sometimes I have this habit of . . ."

"Interfering?"

Palmer smiled. "Well, a lot of the time. But I'm going to be more careful, Amy. I swear it."

Amy's voice softened. "What about Max?" she asked. "I think she deserves an apology, too."

Palmer sighed. "I really didn't think she liked Paul. I mean, she didn't even fight for him when she found out I was writing to him. I didn't think she cared."

"Just because you felt that way doesn't make what you did okay," Amy told her.

"I know," Palmer said quietly. "And I'm going to do something about it right now. I'm going to apologize to Max. I can't stand having her mad at me."

For the first time Amy smiled. "Well, I guess I should apologize for some of the things I said. I haven't exactly been an angel. Besides, impossible as you are, I've missed you."

"Me, too!" Palmer said, and nearly knocked her roommate off the bench with a hug.

Back at the stands, Palmer searched wildly for Max. She found Shanon and Mars, but Max wasn't with them. Maybe she was with Muffin Talbot. Palmer covered every row of bleachers, but there was no sign of Max anywhere. *Maybe Max didn't even come to the game*, Palmer thought. *Maybe she is so depressed she just stayed in the suite.* Palmer wanted to talk to Paul Grant and make sure Germaine didn't tell him any more lies about her, but she knew she had to find Max first. She was beginning to understand just how rough the last few weeks had been for Max—and she felt terrible for her part in it.

Palmer gave the bleachers one last scan, then left the softball field, heading back toward Fox Hall. She was about halfway to the dorm when she saw Max—standing under an oak tree, talking to Paul Grant.

All right, Palmer said to herself. *This is one apology that will have to wait. I've interfered in Max's life for the last time.* She turned and headed back toward the game.

Max stared at the ground, noticing that an ant was crawling along the edge of Paul Grant's sneaker. She'd decided that she wasn't going to the game. She knew Paul was going to be there with Palmer, and she knew she couldn't take seeing that. But as she'd sat in 3-D, trying to write to Jose, she'd realized she couldn't miss Amy's final game. So she'd decided to go, keep her eyes on the field only, and leave the second the game was over.

111

Halfway there, she'd bumped into Paul Grant. Alone. He said that Shanon had told him she was in the dorm. He said he was looking for her, though he hadn't quite figured out how he'd manage to get into Fox Hall. She'd let him stumble through the whole explanation, and she hadn't been able to say a word. And now here she was, staring at an ant, clueless about what to say to him.

"Mars told me not to pay any attention to your letter," Paul rambled on, sounding as nervous as she felt. "He said that you're not really like that, and that something weird was going on."

Max felt herself blush. This whole thing was so embarrassing.

"Is that true?" Paul asked. "Max?" Now his voice was gentle and amused. "How about, just for starters, you look at me. Please?"

Max swallowed hard and looked up—and saw all the warmth in his eyes that she'd remembered from the Valentine's Day Dance. She hadn't imagined it. It was still there, just for her.

"So," Paul said, smiling now, "do you really hate me?"

Max shook her head, feeling herself smile back at him.

"Good." He nodded, as if there was a solemn understanding between them. "Next question: Do you speak?" he teased gently. "English perhaps?"

Max nodded. "Nearly fluent."

"We're making progress. Now, would you please tell me what I did to make you so mad?"

"It wasn't you," Max confessed. "It was Palmer. And me, too, a little." And then she told him about how nervous she'd been after his first letter and about Palmer's deception.

Paul listened quietly. When the story was done he sank down against the tree. "First of all," he said, not looking at her, "you should know I didn't write that first letter. I was so nervous about writing to you that I got a guy in my dorm to do it for me."

"You did?" Max asked, delighted that Paul hadn't written that mushy note. He'd been nervous about her, too!

"Secondly," he went on in a bitter tone, "I feel like a world-class jerk. I can't believe I fell for Palmer's trick."

"Don't feel bad," Maxie said, sitting down beside him. "That's just the way Palmer is." She looked at him out of the corner of her eye. "Are you really one of my father's fans?"

Paul grimaced. "I've never even watched his show. That guy in my dorm, who wrote the first letter, he was the one who told me about Christina Jean Queen. He did this horrendous imitation and then actually taught me how to do it, so I could impress you."

Max laughed until tears came out of her eyes. "I have an idea," she said when she'd caught her breath again. "Maybe—if we keep Palmer and that guy in your dorm out of things—we might actually become pen pals or something."

"Or something," Paul agreed.

Then, before Max knew it was going to happen, he gave her a light kiss on the cheek.

Max was grinning as she left history class. Mr. Seganish had given her another detention, and she didn't even care. Her teacher was right—she hadn't been paying attention. She'd been reliving every moment of Saturday afternoon. Her mind lingered on Paul's first kiss—and all the fun

113

they'd had together. She and Paul had gone to the game and watched as Amy and her teammates brought in the championship victory against Brier Hall. There was so much cheering and confetti Max had thought the bleachers were going to explode. Paul had told her he thought she looked very romantic with confetti in her hair. And then after the game, Palmer had caught up with her, apologizing like mad. Feeling generous toward the whole world, Max had readily forgiven her.

Now as she neared Fox Hall, she realized that for the first time in a while she was actually looking forward to returning to 3-D. This evening the Foxes were going to wrap Dan and Maggie's present, which had been delivered Saturday while they were watching the game.

"Excuse me, miss," said a polite but familiar voice.

Max looked up, unable to believe her eyes. "Paul, what are you doing here? How'd you get a pass for the middle of the week?"

"Special circumstances," he said mysteriously.

"What special circumstances?"

"If you'll follow me," he said, nodding toward the back of Fox Hall.

"Anytime, anywhere," Max murmured, falling into step beside him.

She followed him around the back of the building. Paul led her to a medium-sized cardboard box, and sketched a half bow.

"For me?" Max squeaked. She'd only really known him two days. Was it possible he was bringing her a present already?

"Not exactly," Paul said, laughter in his eyes. "But you're definitely the one who should open it."

114

Max knelt beside the box, her heart pounding. She heard a small scuffling noise inside. "Oh," Max moaned, "it couldn't be . . ."

"Open it," Paul said softly.

Max threw open the box. And Gracie Grayson-Griffith leaped into her arms!

Max held the squirming dog, feeling tears run down her cheeks, onto its white fur. "Oh, Gracie," she sobbed.

The little dog gave a happy yip and licked her tears away.

At last Max looked up at Paul. "How did you—where—"

"Yesterday morning I was jogging down by the river. And I saw this wet little ball of fur. I went to investigate, and saw that she was hurt. She was such a mess. I wasn't even sure if it was Gracie."

For the first time Max noticed a bandage around Gracie's hind leg.

"Anyway," Paul went on, "I brought her back to Ardsley, and we talked our faculty dorm resident into driving us into Brighton to this twenty-four-hour veterinary clinic. The vet kept her overnight for observation. He said she had a nasty gash and was a little dehydrated, but she'll be fine."

Max hugged the little dog even tighter. "We've got to get her to Maggie and Dan."

"You go," Paul said, suddenly sounding shy. "I mean—I don't know them or anything and—"

"No problem," Max said, taking his arm. "Now is the perfect time to introduce you."

The four Foxes stood gathered around the teddy bear that Max had bought.

115

"I know we agreed on a giant bear," Shanon said, "but did it have to be this big? How are we ever going to wrap this thing?"

"I don't care!" Max said blissfully. "All is right in the universe, and there isn't a problem that can touch me."

"She's lost her mind," Amy said fondly.

"No, she's just boy crazy," Palmer said.

"*And* Gracie's back!" Max reminded them, falling backward onto the loveseat. "Don't forget Gracie."

"How could we?" Shanon asked. "You haven't talked about anything else for the last three hours."

"Except for a few speeches about Paul Grant," Amy added.

"He's wonderful," Max said in a dreamy voice.

"We know!" the other three shouted at once.

Max sat up. "All right," she said briskly. "I say we get out all those leftover rolls of crepe paper that have been sitting in the closet since who knows when, and use them to wrap the bear. We'll never find a piece of paper that's big enough."

"She still functions," Amy marveled.

Shanon went to the closet and began tossing out rolls of brightly colored crepe paper. Palmer immediately selected one that was powder blue and began to wrap the bear's right arm. Shanon chose bright yellow for his middle, and Amy began a purple turban. Max stretched out a piece of green, wondering where she should start.

The door to the suite swung open and Georgette bopped in, her blond hair in a ponytail.

"Don't bother knocking or anything," Palmer muttered.

"Guess what?" Georgette said.

"What?" Shanon asked politely.

"I brought mail."

Palmer put her hands on her hips. "What are *you* doing with the mail for this suite?"

Georgette looked innocent. "It was put in my box by mistake. I guess they thought one Durand was like another."

"You wish," Palmer said sweetly.

Georgette made a big production of searching through her shoulder bag and then finally drew out two letters and a postcard. "Postcard from R. Blackburn for Palmer and letter from Smith for Amy. Since I already had Palmer's postcard, I decided to pick up the mail for the rest of 3-D."

"Smith?" Shanon said. "Who's that? Have you been holding out on us, Amy?"

"Not that I know of," Amy said, opening the letter curiously.

Dear Amy,

I hope you don't mind my writing to you like this, but I heard that you and your roommates were into pen pals. Mostly, I wanted to tell you that I watched your last three games and I think you're incredible. You make softball more exciting than major league baseball.

Just so you have an idea about who I am, here are the basic facts: I'm from Greece, originally, but my family moved to the U.S. when I was two, and I grew up in New Orleans. I'm in my third year at Ardsley, taking a lot of science and art—science to shut up my parents, and art 'cause it's what I really love. I've known I wanted to paint since I was three.

Then there's this new interest I've developed—watching the catcher on Alma's softball team. The only problem is the season's over, so I don't know when I'll get to see her again.

Maybe you'll write back to me and we'll get a chance to get to know each other. If not, that's okay. It's been terrific watching you play. Thanks for the great games.

Sincerely,
Nikos Smith

"Sounds like Amy's got a new pen pal," Shanon teased.

"Maybe," Amy said, but she was smiling. She looked at Palmer. "Rain wrote to you?"

Palmer examined the postcard, surprised and pleased. It was a Renoir painting of a girl with long, wavy golden hair.

Dear Palmer,

I saw this painting in the museum and couldn't figure out why I kept staring at it until I realized she reminded me of you. I've been thinking—maybe I will take a trip up to New Hampshire sometime soon.

Write back soon,
Rain

"He thinks you look like a Renoir!" Georgette squealed.

For once Palmer didn't say a word. It was hard to tell from just one postcard, but it sounded like Rain Blackburn might be having a change of heart.

"Can I see the postcard again?" Georgette asked, holding out her hand. "My hair is sort of like that when I wear it down."

Palmer eyed her stepsister suspiciously. "There's one letter you haven't given us. Who's it for?"

"Me," said Georgette. "It's from Sam O'Leary. He's my pen pal now."

"That figures," said Palmer.

"You've got Rain now," Max pointed out.

"True," Palmer agreed, smiling, "but I may need another one who lives closer." There was a silence and she added, "But not someone who's already taken. I promise!"

"Come on," said Max, picking up the green crepe paper again. "We've got a bear to wrap."

Later that night Max grinned as she took out a photograph of her father. "To my favorite fan, Paul Grant," she wrote across the bottom. "Thanks for all your wonderful letters. Can't wait to see your Christina Jean Queen."

She signed it Max, and laughed as she sent it off to her new pen pal.

Something to write home about . . .
                          another new Pen Pals story!

In Book 17, THE BOY PROJECT, there's a new boy—on the Alma Stephens campus! Fen Hudson arrives from the nearby Pewter School for Boys to write an article about life at a girls' school—and Shanon gets to videotape his visit! What a thrill for Shanon! The cutest boy in the world has just zoomed into her life on a motorcycle. Every letter her pen pal Mars writes her says the same old, boring thing. Could it be that Mars is history in Shanon's book? Shanon and Fen are a hot item for now—but what about 4-ever?

AWESOME NEWS!
MICHELLE GOT HER NAME
IN A PEN PALS BOOK!

Michelle Forrest from Wichita, Kansas, wrote PEN PALS headquarters and told us about herself and her pen pal Susie Goldstein from Atlanta, Georgia. The two girls have been writing to each other ever since they were matched up—way back in August! Guess what? Michelle and Susie are both Scorpios. And Susie helped Michelle name her new kitten, Purrfect!

Congratulations, Michelle! Check out page 109 in book #16, *Boy Crazy,* and you'll find that a character has been named after you. The character named Michelle is an outfielder, Amy's best friend on the softball team. Don't thank us, Michelle. Thank Sharon Dennis Wyeth for making your name famous!

Every month, Sharon Dennis Wyeth, the author of the PEN PALS series, names a character in one of her books after a PEN PALS reader. If you'd like to have a character named after you, write in and let us know what's going on with you and your pen pal. What do you guys actually *say* in your letters? Are you making any exciting plans to call or visit your pen pals?

Don't write back soon, write now! Send your letters to:

PEN PALS HEADQUARTERS
c/o PARACHUTE PRESS
156 FIFTH AVE. ROOM 325
NEW YORK, NY 10010

People *really do* get Pen Pals! The pen pals you'll read about below are having a ball writing to one another. So get into the act—don't let these kids have all the fun!

Shannon Balentine of Caribou, Maine, is writing to Nicole Gagnon of Prince George, British Columbia, Canada.

Anna Riggs of Collinsville, Virginia, is writing to Amy Fowler of North Ogden, Utah.

Jari Burnmester of Vancouver, Washington, is writing to Terri Bergeson of Estherville, Iowa.

Amy Pappafava of Lower Burrell, Pennsylvania, is writing to Melissa Kiscoan of Omaha, Nebraska.

Sarah Smith of Salinas, California, is writing to Anna M. Tracey of Las Vegas, Nevada.

Kaymarie Knapp of Shoreham, New York, is writing to Kristin Lundgren of Nattydale, New York.

You can have your very own pen pal, too. All you have to do is fill out the form at the end of this book and send it in. We want to find you the perfect pen pal ASAP!

WANTED: BOYS — AND GIRLS —
WHO CAN WRITE !

Join the Pen Pals Exchange and get a pen pal of your own!

Fill out the form below.

Send it with a self-addressed stamped envelope to:

PEN PALS EXCHANGE
c/o The Trumpet Club
PO Box 632
Holmes, PA 19043
U.S.A.

In a couple of weeks you'll receive the name and address of someone who wants to be your pen pal.

Cut here --

PEN PALS EXCHANGE

NAME _____ GRADE _____

ADDRESS _____

TOWN _____ STATE _____ ZIP _____

DON'T FORGET TO INCLUDE A STAMPED ENVELOPE
WITH YOUR NAME AND ADDRESS ON IT!

Please check one
☐ I bought this book in a store.
☐ I bought this book through the Trumpet Book Club.

Look for your name in PEN PALS books. We'll pick names of matched up Pen Pals every month to print right in a PEN PALS book.